homeward
to ithaka

LEONARD WIBBERLEY

homeward
to ithaka

WILLIAM MORROW AND COMPANY, INC.
NEW YORK 1978

Printed in the United States of America.

1   2   3   4   5   6   7   8   9   10

Library of Congress Cataloging in Publication Data

Wibberley, Leonard Patrick O'Connor (date)
    Homeward to Ithaka.

        I. Title.
PZ4.W632Ho   1978   [PS3573.I2]   813'.5'4   77-11984
ISBN 0-688-03266-4

BOOK DESIGN   CARL WEISS

foreword

THIS BOOK, AS IS USUAL WITH MY WORK, WENT ON ITS OWN
way, and that way was by no means the road I had mapped
out for it. I had intended to take the mass of material surrounding the Ulster hero Cúchulainn and those associated
with him—Conchobor, the wizard Cathbad, the warrior Conall Cernach and so on—and weave it all into a historical
novel. It is marvelous rich material. Read a line or two of it
in translation and one can almost hear the thundering rumble
of the charging war chariots, smell the sweat of horses and
warriors, see the flash of spear, shield and sword and feel the
earth tremble as two armies fall on each other. It is hard

not to be stirred by such material as is contained in the *Táin Bo Cuailnge* (*The Cattle Raid of Cooley*—one of the principal tales concerning the Irish hero Cúchulainn)—and I think it was Matthew Arnold who pointed out with some excitement that the Irish myths were almost as rich as those of ancient Greece.

I decided to start the story in New York, with a professor of comparative literature at Columbia transported back to Cúchulainn's times. But I had hardly commenced when the enchantress Circe walked in, and then Ulysses himself. So the story of Cúchulainn got mixed up with the struggle of Ulysses to return to Penelope and Ithaka, and with the need of the professor to find his own true home also. The material, in short, took over from me and gave the direction and the detail to the book. My part was to endure a powerful hallucination until it was all over.

Those who are authorities on the Irish myths will find much to quarrel with in this novel, where I have taken some well-known incidents and used them in another context. They may object to my placing the Cúchulainn story in Bronze Age times —roughly 2500 B.C. in Ireland. I did so because myths are not history, but the glimmer of history, and also because I was so powerfully impressed by the passage graves at New Grange and Knowth and by the splendid display of Bronze Age weapons and jewelry in the National Museum in Dublin. Some hold that Cúchulainn's period should be much closer to the Christian era. Some hold that the stories surrounding Cúchulainn are not really ancient, but were fabricated in the seventh or eighth century by monks to provide Ireland with a mythology that might match that of Greece. But if this is so, they must have worked on old pagan mythology. I doubt any group of men or any one man had the power of mind and imagination to produce such tremendous tales out of nothing. Cúchulainn may never have existed in the flesh. But someone like him and the figures surrounding him must certainly have existed. They are as real as Hector, Achilles, Agamemnon and Ulysses himself.

The sources of my Irish material are many, and I mention only those I chiefly used. There was, first of all, the splendid translation of the *Táin* by the poet Thomas Kinsella and entitled simply *The Tain* (Oxford). This is a work of love, of scholarship, of years and of honesty, so that the tendency to make things "nice" in other translations is scrupulously avoided and the people and actions of the story are presented frankly and in full color. Much not in *The Tain* itself I found explained and enlarged in Professor Proinsias MacCana's *Celtic Mythology* (Hamlyn) and to round out the top trio of my Irish sources there was *Celtic Heritage. Ancient Tradition in Ireland and Wales* by Alwyn Rees and Brinley Rees (Grove Press). There were many other sources of varying importance to me— *Irish Sagas*, edited by Myles Dillon (Mercier), *The Irish before the Conquest*, by Lady Ferguson (George Bell and Sons. The book is now out of print), and *Antiquities of the Irish Countryside*, by Sean P. O'Riordain (Methuen), among them. The names given to weapons I got very largely from Kinsella—and some of the translations too. Others I worked out with the use of Dineen's *Irish-English Dictionary*. True enough, the dictionary is in modern Irish, but it is of great use in making an intelligent guess at the meanings of some early Irish names.

As I have taken liberties with the Homeric epic in creating an adventure of Ulysses unknown to the Greeks, so I have taken a liberty with the Irish myth, melding into one the personages of Fergus Mac Roich, King of Ulster, and Fergus Mac Roth, leader of the host of Connaught. This was done to give a needed drive and unity to the story as I have told it. Also I have used throughout the name of the smith Culann in the genitive case—Chulainn—to give a closer affinity with Cúchulainn, the boy-warrior who became his Hound.

As for Ulysses, I did not make my own translation of the verses given. I used instead the appealing translation of Robert Fitzgerald, *Homer. The Odyssey* (Anchor Press/Doubleday), as my basic material, and rewrote the incidents to my own taste—giving, I trust, a Greek flavor—but without pentameters.

What is it, then, when it is all put together? It is a fantasy based on myths from two widely separated cultures, but having, I do believe, some solid bearing on life as we live it or occasionally catch glimpses of it.

LEONARD WIBBERLEY

Hermosa Beach,
California

pRelude

---

hear now the song of Ulysses,
    Master of sea ways and trackless wastes,
    Son of great Laertes and the ancient gods:
    How when he left the smoking ruins of Troy,
    Burned wood, burned flesh and burning hate behind,
He launched his black-hulled ships from that dread beach
On which they'd lain nine long years or more.
Smiting the purple sea with their long oars
His crew cried, "Ithaka and home—at last we come."

Thus they took the seas and, homeward bound,

Each oar's tug a weight from off their hearts,
So long they'd been away from hearth and farm,
While on Olympian heights Zeus,
Lord of clouds and all the gods,
Smiled.
For well he knew no ferry passage home
Awaited Ulysses or his crew.

First then there rose above the cresting waves,
Azure and frosted silver 'neath the wind,
The strong blue line of Kikones' rugged coast,
With here and there a smear of golden sun
Touching a mountain flank beyond.
                                          A fair city,
Ismaros, strongly held, was soon in view and
Ulysses smiled to think of plunder waiting
If one swift raid he dared. The ships swung in.
The men leaped out waist-deep into
The swirling seas. Plunder they took—
Sheep, cattle, wine and women. Then
Came horsemen leather-clad, an army trained
That fell on them and cut them down.
Back to their ships they fought and on the stones
Left groaning dying and red-painted dead
Snatched with a spear's thrust or an ax's blow
From the bright world of laughing waves and sun
To gloomy Hades of eternal shade.
Such the price
For one miscast of war's uncertain dice.

Then Zeus raised a storm upon the seas,
A blackened northern wind of iron weight.
Sails ripped to tatters, e'en the yards were down,
Flapping in mighty gusts in the white gale.

Out oars then, and every man
Pulled till his tendons cracked
Against the howling wind and roaring seas.
Three days of this. Then calm and then again
They ran, bare-poled, rigging strained, before a wind,
Death-chill,
That made a seething caldron of the sea.
At last they came to that summering land
Where live the Lotus Eaters.
"Taste of these blooms," they said, "gaunt, sea-rimed men.
They banish sorrow, pain, all memory
Of duty, work, toil, misery and stress.
One taste and every trouble gone. Nothing remains
But dreamy present in the fragrant air."
Some reached with worn and sea-cracked hands for blooms,
But wily Ulysses, so quick of mind,
Thrust them back.
                    "Eat nothing, shipmates all," he said,
"Or you'll become like these—the living dead,
Smiling mindless and pretending life.
Surely your homes, your families, your friends,
The nip of frost, the scouring of the wind,
The lowing of your cattle in the sheds,
The clump of spade and smell of new-turned earth
Are dearer far to you than dreaming nothingness.
Think hard of that. Back to the ships."

                                        They left

Though many, straining at the oars
And thinking of the long sea-miles ahead,
Yearned for the Lotus and an end to care.
Next, in the night's silent and cold sea fog,
Gray air upon gray water lying close
With not a stir in sea or mist above,

They came upon an island and, wafted in
By some benevolent god, beached ships
And slept until the dawn. Then found
The island thick with goats, with barley bright,
Grape vines, grain of every kind
Growing wild.
It was the Cyclops' Isle they'd come upon.
Monsters of one eye and minds so dull,
They knew not how to plow or raise the crops
Or build a house or slender high-prowed ships.
Like beasts they were, all living solitary,
Each in his own cave on the land beyond.
Now there went Ulysses with one sole ship
To spy upon them, find out how they lived,
What were their entertainments and their joys.
Nothing would bar that man from venturing.
Danger he loved second only to his home.
They beached the ship and came upon the cave
of Polyphemos, Lord Poseidon's son,
Brother to Zeus and maker of earthquakes
And great storms at sea.

                                        In they went

And found plentiful around, great cheeses
And big bowls of milk.
To take the cheeses, two apiece, and run
Would have been discreet. But Ulysses,
A moth forever circling danger's flame,
Must wait to see the owner of the cave.
He came too soon, a shambling hairy hill
Of living flesh, and drove his flocks
Of purple-fleeced sheep into the cave,
Then rolled a great stone of a ship's full weight
Into the entrance, entombing them.
Next he sparked a fire and as the flames

Slashed dark away, he spied the men.
Quick as a cat he picked up two of them
And chomped them screaming in his hairy jaws,
Nor heeded any plea for mercy.
The same he did upon the following night.
But Ulysses, that man of many schemes,
Had found a pole thick as a coaster's mast
Within the cave. One end he sharpened,
Hardened in the fire. "This will serve," he said,
"To blind the eye of that man-eating lout."
When next the Cyclops came, the schemer greeted him
With cordial words. "I have with me,"
He said, "a precious wine that gives great zest
To meat. Come, drink your fill.
Brandy it's called, and you should be warned
It's strong stuff. Too much and your head will spin,
And all good sense seep swiftly out of it."
Three bowls the scornful Cyclops drank and then,
Fuddled and thick-tongued,
Stumbled and crashed drunken to the ground.
Then Ulysses heated once again
His sharpened pole in the glowing fire,
Summoned his men, and drove the flaming point,
Hissing and steaming, into the Cyclops' eye.
Round they turned it and drove it deeper still
While blood and steam and ooze came rolling out.
The Cyclops screamed and shook the cave with roars,
Seized the pole and pulled it from his eye,
And, blinded, groped raging here and there
But found not one of Ulysses' stout crew.
The master schemer then bound his men
Beneath the bellies of the fatted sheep
With twisty osiers from the ogre's bed.
Ulysses clung leechlike to the fleece

Of a sturdy ram and so awaited
Rosy-fingered dawn
And their release
From that dung-deep cave.

When at last the baa-ing of the flocks
Told the groaning Cyclops he must move
The giant stone from the cavern door,
Out went the sheep,
The men beneath, Ulysses last of all.
Sweet the sea breeze to their gasping lungs.
Quickly they were freed and found the ship
Driving the Cyclops' wondrous sheep ahead.

So aboard.
                            The long oars bit the waves
And Ulysses, savoring sweet revenge,
Beyond the surf line raised his taunting shout,
"Hi, Cyclops! Polyphemos! Eater of men!
Hear now the name of him who put out
That great light centered in your ugly head.
Ulysses I am, the great Laertes' son,
Whose home's in Ithaka. Yes, it was I,
Roaming the lone seas,
Who blinded you with my sizzling pole,
Down to Hell I'd take you if I could."

Then Polyphemos with a thunder shout
Broke off a hilltop with one hand and hurled
The mass of it straight at the rolling ship.
It fell ahead and the huge wave it raised
Drove Ulysses' ship ashore.
                            Off they pushed
And with a racing stroke pulled farther out.

Again Ulysses renewed his taunt,
Mocking that blinded beast-man on the shore.
Polyphemos raised his hands to Heaven,
Praying his father, the mighty Lord Poseidon,
That Ulysses should never feel again
The earth of Ithaka beneath his feet,
Or, if he did, that all who went with him
Should die upon the seaward track.
Poseidon heard that prayer, and answered swift.
For soon they came into a bay all walled about with stone,
Upon an island strange,
And nary boat nor boatman to be found.
Here lived the Laistrygones, eaters of men,
Who, pelting boulders from unerring slings,
Sank all the ships but one and ate the crew,
Floating like gutted herring in the sea.
Ulysses' ship pulled free and, sailing thence,
Was wafted to the shore of Circe's Isle,
Enchantress beautiful and dread who turned his men,
Sun-bronzed and strong, into grunting swine,
All with one draft of drugged Pramnian wine.

Warned by Hermes, Ulysses escaped.
(The gods love well a brave and cunning man.)
The god told Ulysses that he must eat
A certain plant of magic, black the root
And white the flower—*molu* its name,
And so escape enchantment.

                           Then Circe, marveling,
Loved the bold seafarer and restored
His men to their own shape and human form,
Befriended him, and in her perfumed bed
Gave him her love in nights of soft delight,

And warned him of the hazards still ahead
Between her golden shore and Ithaka:
How he must visit first the Land of Death
And from great Tiresias get his course
Across the fish-filled seas to his own home.
Lashed to his mast he must pass the Sirens,
Luring him to death, his men's ears stopped
With plugs of beeswax while they worked the oars.
Over the long ocean swells.

Then dead ahead
They'd find the Drifting Rocks, foam-slashed and grim,
That neither bird nor ship could ever pass
Unless the gods gave leave. Another course thereafter
He should take between two headlands dour—
The one a mountain peaking to the clouds,
Its sides so sheer no man might master them.
Here dwelt at half the mountain's slippery height
Six-headed yapping Skylla who must snatch
Six of his crew to feed her cruel maw.
Across the strait, beneath a vast wild fig,
Lay Charybdis, the suckhole of the seas,
Three times each day swallowing down the tide
And three times vomiting it back again.
"Take the Skylla coast," the goddess said.
"Six men you'll lose. There is no help for it.
But Charybdis will suck into its maw
Ship's oars, mast, sails and all the crew.
A total loss. No need for one like you
To weigh such odds.
But drive the rowers hard or twelve, not six,
Skylla will snatch from off the rowing bench.
"These dangers passed, one further yet remains.
Trinakria island soon will loom ahead
Where graze the sacred Cattle of the Sun,

The herds of Helios.

Land not there.

Or, landing, do not touch a single one
Of those sleek beasts, for if you do,
All will perish and you alone be left,
Solitary and old, still seeking Ithaka."
So the goddess warned.

Then the black ship,
Provisioned, caulked, all her gear restored,
Breasted the wine-dark sea and all fell out
As Circe had foretold.

But when at last
The Land of Death, the Sirens, Skylla, Charybdis,
All were passed (six men they lost
To Skylla's yapping mouths)
Ahead rose Trinakria, island of delight,
Of pleasant coves and gleaming sea-lapped bays.
No words of Ulysses could stop his crew
From sheltering there.

"Great Zeus, do you think our arms are iron,
Hauling and pulling at these leaden oars
By light and dark? Sun-scorched, then shivering
In the night's fierce spray?" So Eurylokhos cried—
He who'd stood by Ulysses in every strait.
The others backed him up, they'd row no more
But rest in quiet waters by the shore
Of Trinakria.

Laertes' son, far-ranging Ulysses,
First made each rower swear a mighty oath
To leave the Sun God's sacred beasts alone.
Each took the oath, then turned the ship aside

((17))

And beached her on a shore of softest sand,
Fringed with flowers and sweet-smelling vines.
That night a mighty wind from off the sea
Screamed shoreward, raising walls of thundering surf.
A month it blew, and all provisions spent,
Even the oxhide rigging boiled for food,
Eurylokhos eyed the sleek beeves around,
Chewing their cuds in the lush, flowering grass.
"Mates," he said. "Since starving men must die,
And broken oaths they say will bring death too,
Let's die full-bellied. Come. What do you say?
Already I can taste the good hot tripes
Of that sleek heifer grazing on the hill."

They killed the beast, flayed, split and quartered it
And, skinny-armed, put the bleeding joints
Upon the fire. Falling to,
They crammed their mouths with dripping flesh and fat.
Then Ulysses, who'd gone inland to pray,
Returned and found the sacrilege.

He faced each man in anger, nose to nose,
Denounced their folly, said their deaths were sure.
They shrugged. Since men must die, why starve?
They said, but cringed to see
The cowhide crawling over the soft sand
Toward the summering grass.
The wind died. The roaring, storming surf
Turned to ripples fit for children's play.
They launched, rigged mast, yard and sail,
Set seaward, marveling.

But when the last gray smear of land was gone
A storm cloud gathered monstrous overhead.

Great gusts of wind piled waves half mast-high.
The forestays went, the yard came crashing down.
The mast too, splitting the helmsman's skull,
The first to die. Bolt after bolt
Great Zeus flung from out the thundercloud.
Stem to stern the black-hulled ship was split.
Great waves engulfed the men and drowned them all
Save Ulysses.

                  He, clinging to the hulk,
Saw her great keel break off and float up free,
So lashed it to the yard and splintered mast.
A raft he made to weather out the storm
And yet was washed (Poseidon hated him)
Back to the suckhole of the restless seas
To Charybdis.

               The vortex opened wide,
Black, glittering, and took him down through Time
And Space,
Then spewed him up but in another place,
Demented, changed, not knowing who he was,
Groping and lost, nor scarcely could recall
His home and wife in stony Ithaka. . . .

CHAPTER

1

HE CIRCUMSTANCES OF THE START WERE UTTERLY ordinary—completely without promise of anything at all. Most of that bleak day I had been teaching Comparative Literature to students at Columbia who did not care to learn much about Comparative Literature. They had been advised, or compelled, to take the course to get their degrees, and so they cared only for their grades. I could not blame them, yet I resented them.

I did my best, that leaden, freezing afternoon, to relieve the polished, affected grace of eighteenth-century English literature by switching to the stark, muscular, bloody prose of the Irish myths, in particular the *Táin Bo Cuailnge—The Cattle Raid of Cooley*—when the whole of the Kingdom of Connaught—horses, chariots, spears, battle axes, shields, swords and sweating warriors out for heads—had launched itself against the Kingdom of Ulster, the spoils being a brown bull. There was a spark of interest for a moment from the class, but nothing more, not even when I pointed to the parallel cattle-raiding exploits of the ancient Greeks as touched on in Homer and the cattle raiding in the American West a hundred years ago.

From somewhere in the back of the class I heard the word *baloney;* and since it is modern dogma that only teachers fail and students never, I had obviously failed.

When that purgatory was done, when I had been sharp with some of them and then repented my sharpness and the whole lecture shambles was over, I had the kind of headache that I recognize as the symptom of an approaching and unavoidable state of mind.

I went then immediately to my office, locked the door and lay down among the piles of books in which I have lived a thousand lives more vivid than my present daily life. Unless you are born again, you cannot enter the Kingdom of Heaven. How true. Books are my baptism. But for many of my students there were merely grades. Most of them would never know rebirth. To be born again. . . . What comfort.

The college provided the desk and the chairs in my office. The couch was mine. It was rumored that on the couch I seduced selected female students in return for which they got good grades. I had occasionally the desire, but never the courage. My proper epitaph should be "Through fear, he lost delight."

Lying on the couch, my head throbbing, I waited for the relief, listening to the ticking of a clock given me by my parents and to the slight wheezing in my chest which resulted from asthma. Both sounds were consoling.

I looked up at the ceiling. In the electric light it showed pale blue. Then it became a summer sky and I a boy lying on my back looking up at it in dreamy delight in a New England meadow. The transformation was complete, and I dreamed the dreams that boy had dreamed before he was changed by some spell into a man.

I felt with great conviction that I should do now what I had believed I would do when I had been that dreaming boy—go to some far exotic island and sit in the sun, barefoot, and look at the sea. I should become a wanderer like the greatest of all wanderers—Ulysses. Was I not born to wander? Was that not my true nature? In a moment I was standing on a beach of gray pebbles, watching Ulysses and his men.

They smote with their oars the wine-dark sea . . .

How that line had gripped me when I first read it, like hearing a familiar phrase, long forgotten, called out again. I could see the oars. They were of pale gold, like the wood of the yew cut in winter. The looms were long and narrow and bent under the strain of the rowers. When the blades struck the sea, they flung cascades of silver into the air. The sun gilded the muscles of the men's shoulders and thighs as they strained against the suck, and the black hollow ship rose groaning over the scending sea.

There was a knock at the door. It shattered Ulysses, his ship, the island, the purple sea and the silver-crested waves— and a part of myself which is continually destroyed, only to be born again.

"Come in," I said.

The enchantress Circe entered. She had about her the fragrance of lime blossoms. Her eyes were toffee soft, and her young breasts were smooth and full under a pink sweater.

((22))

They were swollen with desire, for I could see the nipples push out the pink wool. An enchantress, she wore no bra.

"Is it too late to turn in my paper on Gray?" she asked. "I was sick yesterday."

She glanced at the couch.

> *Then Ulysses, the man of cunning, said to Circe,*
> *"Don't think you can entice me to your lovely bed.*
> *When you have stripped my clothing away*
> *You will reach with tender questing fingers*
> *And unman me, and take away my daring. . . ."*

"Yes," I said. "It will be all right."

She closed the door quietly and sat on the couch. "Let's make love," she said.

> *"First," said Ulysses, "you must swear a mighty oath that*
> *You will leave me whole and as I am*
> *And try no shameful tricks on me."*

"No," I said. "Not because you are not desirable, but if we did and you told anyone, which you probably would, my reputation would be ruined."

"I won't talk, I swear," she said. "Cross my heart." She did so. Then she kicked off her platform shoes and struggled out of her blue jeans. She wore white panties. Her thighs were round and her buttocks firm and small. When she lay on the couch I could see the breathtaking shadow of her pubic hair. It was jet black. I slipped my hands up under her sweater to explore her breasts with trembling fingers. She moaned and wriggled out of her panties and I undid my belt. She embraced me slowly with her arms and thighs, her mouth open and gentle as a rose. She was ready immediately, demanding my love. When we were done, I did not want to withdraw, but she pushed me gently away.

"I have a train to catch," she said. "To the Bronx."

"Let us lie a little while so," I pleaded.

"Tomorrow," she replied.

> *Then Circe slipped on a shimmering gown*
> *Made of star stuff, I am sure, and sheer*
> *As moonstones. A precious girdle*
> *She cast about her comely waist. . . .*

Only it was white panties and blue jeans that she put on, followed by her platform shoes.

"See you," she said, and was gone.

I looked at the paper on Gray. She had left (a love gift?) a little packet of mistletoe, for it was near Christmas. The paper was a disaster. She had confused Gray with Goldsmith and said Goldsmith had written a poem about a graveyard outside an English hamlet—called "The Deserted Village." But then Circe had no need of eighteenth-century English poets, so I gave her an *A*.

Her name at this time, I noted from the top of her paper, was Deirdre Connor. I returned to the couch, hoping to re-join Ulysses and his men, but they had gone. Instead, Circe— disguised as Deirdre Connor, a student at Columbia—insisted on intruding. I said the name *Deirdre* several times, thinking of Derdriu of the Sorrows and then "Connor" until it changed into another name *Conchobor*—Conchobor of Emain Macha, mighty and golden-bearded, gray-eyed, his face strong but with a touch of simpleness. Yet it was the face of a man not quite a fool. I saw him plainly. His robe was silvery, deco-rated with red spirals. Cathbad stood behind him—Cathbad the Druid; his eyes were close set and he smelled of sweat and dried blood. He raised a long bony arm and hand toward me and beckoned. I looked upward at the ceiling, searching for the comfort of the New England sky. It had gone. Instead there was only blackness out of which whirled bitter, tiny particles of snow.

CHAPTER

2

I T WAS COLD BEYOND ENDURANCE AND I WAS STANDING AT
the door of a tenement at the corner of West Eighty-sixth
and Broadway. The lower windows were boarded up and
the place was plainly condemned. I went through the
front door, painted years ago to resemble limed oak. There
was a flight of stairs before me, and I went up them. On the
landing at the top was a window, the glass broken. It opened
up on one of those light shafts, or ventilation shafts, that
are a feature of brick tenements in New York. Through the
window came a dirty stream of light. It was enough to show
me the next flight of stairs.

There were six flights of stairs in all. At the foot of the

last I heard a terrifying sound—a desperate sucking in of air into congested lungs, and then its expulsion, accompanied by a low whistle. Then the terrible, painful sucking again. It came from beyond an apartment door on the top landing. The door was unlocked. I pushed it open. The apartment appeared empty. But in a far corner of a bedroom someone lay struggling for breath on a filthy couch. The poor devil was already in the dark, on his journey to gloomy Hades where wretches live in terrible night without end.

In the dirty evening light I found in the middle of the room a crazy dresser, left by whoever had once lived in this desolate place; on it, in a saucer, was the stub of a candle.

I lit the candle. The flame dimmed as I moved toward him. The light blinded me. I did not see him except as a lump which wheezed and sucked in the darkness.

I put the candle on a box beside the couch. The flame steadied and grew from a blue bud to a golden flower, and a dying man emerged from the darkness like a phantom. His eyes, the rims all red, were sunk into his head. The flesh of his eyebrows drooped over the deep sockets. It was criss-crossed with a thousand tiny wrinkles, like fingernail marks made in putty. His skin had a brown tinge like a withered leaf. His teeth were long and yellow and his thin lips, from which sprouted a few hairs, could not cover them.

He was a mummy.

"Who are you?" I cried.

In the flickering pale gold of the candlelight he reached out his corpse hand to me. "Mistletoe," he said, but the words he used were *uil olc,* which is Gaelic for *mistletoe.*

"Give me the all-healer," he added.

I reached in my pocket for the packet of mistletoe left me by Circe or Deirdre Connor, and gave it to him. He tore the packet open and, taking out the little dryish sprig, he ate it leaves, twig, berries and all. One of the berries fell on the dirty coverings and he picked it up and held it out to me.

"Eat it," he said. "It is the seed of life itself."

In the candlelight that is what it looked like, a globule of spermatozoa. I put it in my mouth.

The moment I had swallowed it an icy mist oozed through the window. I heard strident trumpeting, heavy rumblings of wheels; smelled earth and blood thick as a slaughterhouse and heard shouts. "Conchobor. Conchobor." That name came clear, and a glimpse of a man as big as Herakles in the swirling mist. Then the name *Fergus,* but no appearance—only the mist tinged with red. Then the slashing of swords and grunts, and more shouting. At the end one name rose, shouted from a hundred thousand throats: "Cúchulainn! Cúchulainn! Cúchulainn!"

I stared at the candle flame and it became a woman, young, but with a sharp, cunning face. Her brow was smooth and white as a peeled stick, and her hair was thick as a horse's tail, and red. It reached her waist. She was dressed in a green robe, with over it a ruby cloak edged in gold

Her strong feet were bare. She was a woman well used to being barefoot, though hardly poor, to judge by her dress. She was seated on the steps of a house—steps of green marble which led up to an ample door of oak᾽ studded with iron, the studs painted red and blue. Around her was a garden of roses, pink and white, and larkspur growing very tall. Before her lay a lawn dappled with daisies.

The woman was clipping her toenails. A man clad in purple, with a belt of black horsehide around his waist, came through the beds of larkspur toward her. She did not look up, though she was aware of him. She snipped away and said, busy with the task, "Tell me, Cathbad the Druid, for what is the present hour good? Is it good for beautification, or is it good for hunting, or is it good for dreaming of men?"

"No question easier answered," said Cathbad. He was extremely long-faced, the eyes so close together that at times he was called Uilibhann—the one-eyed.

"What is the answer?" she asked.

"The hour is favorable to the begetting of a king," he replied.

"Is that really so?" she demanded, looking sharply at him.

"I do not lie," he replied.

The woman, Nessa, stopped clipping her toenails. To do her work more perfectly she had pulled her gown up to her waist. The druid eyed her coolly.

"The men are all in the forest hunting the boar," she said. "There is one with bristles on his back stiffer than needles. His tusks would gut a stallion. Ceth is gone and Cernach and Gubhlain and also my father, Horse of the Yellow Heels. When will this hour come again, Cathbad?"

"Never in your lifetime."

"Then you must serve me," she said.

"I am hungry," said Cathbad. "Give me meat and wine first."

"Easily done," she said and, taking his hand, led him into the house. Serving girls put boar's flesh and swan's flesh and the purple wine of the tribes of the Helvetians before him.

"Eat fast," she said. "Then let us go quickly to bed before the good-omened hour is past. How can you eat at such a time?"

"A man should not be weak to sire a king," said the druid.

When he had finished, they went to the bedchamber.

"To be sure you conceive a king," said Cathbad when they lay naked together, "you must be the rider and I the horse." So he lifted her on him so that her red hair fell over his face and her thighs were straddled outside of his and made his entry with ease. When they were done Cathbad rose and said, "The boy you have conceived will be born on the Feast of Othar. When he is weaned bring him to me on the Flat Island."

"I will do that," she said.

"Do not admit any man to you except I give you leave," he

said. "Otherwise your son will be no king."

"That is a hard condition," said Nessa.

"Kingdoms are not to be torn apart and men gutted to satisfy the loves of women," said Cathbad. "Do as I say in this matter."

The flame of the candle returned slowly, and with it the gaunt, bare tenement room on West Eighty-sixth Street and the mummy of a man sucking for air on the filthy couch. His breath was coming more easily, though, and his face was not as desiccated as it had been. The lips had closed over the long yellow teeth and the sunken eyes were not so deep in the sockets. His shreds of hair gleamed a little in the flickering candle flame.

"Who are you?" I asked.

"A better question, of more weight, I'll put to you," he said. "Who are you? You do not know who you are. I will tell you. You are a wanderer lost in time. You have taken a blind road. You are on a journey and have forgotten where you are going. Do you know where you are going, Wanderer?"

"I am not on a journey," I said. "I just live."

"Nothing just lives," he replied. "Not even the earth itself. What name comes to your mind, Wanderer? Say a name."

"Ithaka." It was like one of those psychological tests in which you produce at random any word that occurs to you in response to a signal.

"Ithaka," he repeated. "Home to Ithaka and lost in the wrong place and the wrong time. The world is full of such as you—self-imprisoned because they do not know where they are going and have lost the sense of their identity. Do you want to resume your journey?"

"I do."

For a moment the flame of the candle held steady in its lovely ovoid shape, flowing from serene gold to deeper red at the peak and then to a needle of smoke lancing gracefully into the gloom above. The face of the mummy beyond it seemed waxen and blurred. Then in the center of the flame, where the blue bud of fire bloomed from the wick, a castle appeared—not the castle of fairy stories but the grim bloodied walls of a fortress of grim bloody men. The day was gray and a wind was blowing which shook the skeleton branches of a clump of elms that grew close to the outer battlement. The wind also set a score or more of human heads, suspended by their hair from the battlements, bobbing and turning in the bitter stream of air.

"What is this place?" I asked.

"It is the fortress of Fergus Mac Roth, King of Ulster," said the mummy.

The walls with the grisly heads, all the mouths black, open holes speaking silence, dissolved, and in their place was a huge hall of wood, the pillars supporting the tremendous roof painted in blue, in red, in black, in gold and in green. In the center stood a massive black-bearded man, clad in a white robe with long sleeves, the robe slashed with diagonal lines of red. A two-handed sword, the pommel decorated with a bronze crown, hung down his back. It was so big, the cross guard showed behind his head. His beard commenced at his cheek-bones and descended to his chest, but just above the line of the beard, below the left eye, there was a white scar which cut across his nose, which seemed as a result to be of two misaligned portions. The lower lid of the eye immediately above this scar was pulled down.

With this man was the druid Cathbad whom I had seen before in his purple robe and his horsehide belt, and also the red-haired woman who had been paring her toenails. But the time was some years later, for beside her stood a boy of about seven, with the same thick horselike hair of the mother. His eyes were blue and his limbs big for his age, and he had a bold look to him. He stared without the slightest fear at the black-bearded man. There was a smell in the air of wet animal skins and sour wine.

"What do you want of me here, Cathbad?" said the bearded man. "What plot have you now in your mind?"

"No plot, Fergus Mac Roth," said Cathbad. "It is time for you publicly to assert your right to be King of Ulster."

"Is this something new? I am already King of Ulster," said Fergus.

"You are not truly king until you mate before all your warriors and their women," said Cathbad.

"I have mated many a time before all of my warriors and their women when the wine vats were half empty," said Fergus. "And they have mated in my sight. I will probably mate again with the same delight. What is new about this?"

"This is new to you—that you are to mate with a white mare."

"A white mare—play stallion to a horse?"

"It is the law of Ulster," said Cathbad.

"It is an old law and a foolish one, and one I will not comply with," said Fergus. But he was interested. "How was this done?" he asked.

"Easily told," said Cathbad. "A mare, carefully groomed, was brought to the Great Hall in the presence of all the people. The king—or he who was to be king—crawled to the mare naked and on all fours. Having kissed her hooves and legs and nuzzled her, he mounted her and had intercourse with her. All the warriors and women watched so they could see that he who was to be king was thoroughly capable of this act and the deed fully done. When they were satisfied that true mating had been completed, the mare was killed and flayed and the flesh was cut into pieces. The pieces were put in a caldron and boiled. When this stew was cool enough the king got into the caldron and, using no utensil but his hands, he drank the soup and ate the flesh of the mare so that

((31))

he became one with her. He was then proclaimed king."

The druid paused and then said, "I have a white mare ready for you."

"I am not inclined to this mating," said Fergus. "Let another who claims the kingdom perform it."

"You have not yet seen the mare," said Cathbad. "You will not find her so little to your liking. Here she is—Nessa, whose father is called the Yellow-Heeled Horse."

"This one," said Fergus. "Haven't you heard about her? Cordere, Nuada, Errge, Sencha the Old One, Dubthach— these and a score of others have been giving her treasures and gifts of every kind to get between her thighs, but without success."

"With you, it will be different," said Cathbad.

"And if I plow her valley, that will make me king beyond all dispute?"

"That is the sacred seal that no one dare ignore—mating with a white mare before the host of warriors and their women."

"Do I have to cut her up, boil her, and eat her afterward?" said Fergus.

The woman Nessa looked frightened. Cathbad did not answer.

"Bring in the warriors and their women then," said Fergus. "Let us make a start on this mating. The mood is on me already."

"Before a start is made," said Nessa, reaching for the pin that held her long gown at the shoulder, "there must be a bargain. Queens are not slave girls. You must offer me a gift." She let the shoulder of her gown slip so that she was naked to the waist, where the gown was held by a belt. Her breasts were rounded and firm, standing out full and framed by her long red hair. Fergus cupped one breast in his hand, reaching for her girdle with the other.

"What exchange?" he asked. He leaned toward her. His

pink mouth showed for a moment through the thicket of black hair, and taking the nipple in his lips, he covered her breasts with his black beard. She moved her fingers through his hair, holding his head down to her, and moving her body against his.

"You must promise that my son Conchobor there shall have authority over Ulster for a year," she said. "Promise that. So that he can call his son the son of a king."

"Your breasts are the sweet fountains of Ireland," he muttered.

"Promise," she demanded.

"I promise," said Fergus, pulling her robe down so that she stood naked in the pool of blue silk.

"All must be done properly," said Cathbad. "Both must be naked before the host of warriors, and you are to crawl to her on all fours and nuzzle her."

The boy watched Fergus being stripped as the warriors entered the hall. A space was made in the middle and the women pressed forward to see, more eager than the men.

Nessa stood slender and naked in the circle of squirming men and women and Fergus, naked, crawled toward her on his hands and knees. He licked her feet and then upward to her knees and thighs. She moaned, her eyes shut, her face averted, her hands caressing his back. The boy Conchobor stood watching, unmoved. Nessa sank to her knees and then to all fours.

"Mount," shouted the warriors. "Mount. The mare is ready." Fergus straddled her, and since he was fondling her breasts at the same time, she had to take the whole weight of his vast body.

The boy Conchobor struggled to pick up the sword of Fergus—the giant two-handed blade that belonged only to the king. He dragged it upright before him and smiled at the druid.

CHAPTER

3

HE CANDLE FLAME WENT OUT. THE WICK GLOWED red in the darkness, the glow increased for a second as if the candle were seeking to rekindle itself, then dwindled and faded to nothing. I could smell only the waxy smoke rising from the guttered wick. I was back in the room with the mummy. Or was I? Was the room itself a hallucination like the scenes I had experienced in Bronze Age Ireland?

"Consider Air, Water, and Earth," said the old man. "There is water in air and air in water. There is water and air in earth and earth in air and water. They are different but they are intermingled. Because they are different does not mean that one exists and the other does not exist."

The room became lighter, with the shroud grayness of pre-dawn. Soon it was light enough to see the old man without the candle flame. He was utterly changed. There were no longer the thin lips drawn back over the long yellow teeth, the terrible sagging eyebrows, the red-rimmed eyes sunk deep in their sockets. Instead there was a man in his middle years, the eyes deep set and close together but sparkling with intelligence even in that drabness that pretended to be light. His face was long, the style of it set by a ridge of a nose sharp as the edge of an ax. He had black hair growing past his shoulders and mingling with a black beard that came to his waist. He wore a robe of Tyrrhenian purple. It was Cathbad the Druid who was before me. His smile was slightly mocking.

"The all-healer," he said. "The mistletoe."

He got up from the miserable couch, and I followed him out of that squalid apartment. A soft light came from him so that I could not, for instance, see the distant walls or floors, but only those he stood near. Down the stairs we went, and I counted the flights—six. Twice three. The Celts love a triplicate. The Three Tales of Sorrowful Telling, the Three Sons of Uisliu, the Three Shouts on the Hill, the Three Signs of a Fop, the Three Sources of the World's Increase. . . .

"The womb of a woman, the udder of a cow, the clay of the potter," said Cathbad. We came to that imitation limed-oak front door and went through it. I touched the cold wood with my hand. It was solid, and chilly as marble. The door opened easily and the snow was still falling outside—far more heavily now. The wind howled and moaned, making dark whirls in the white scatter of the tumbling flakes.

But it was not New York that lay about me, but a great plain, snow-covered to a depth of a foot or more, with here and there, as the wind quested about like a hunting dog, flurries and pillars of snow rising into the gray air like phantoms from the grave.

> *Out of Erebos the spirits groped*
> *Young men and those with grizzled heads,*
> *Brides and maidens and the blinded, gashed*
> *Spirits of warriors killed by ax and brazen sword*
> *Gory their gear, and battered their shields. . . .*

"You begin to recall something of yourself," said Cathbad.

There was a hill in the mid-distance—a long ridge of ground with a valley beyond. Over this, through the swirling flakes, now came a troop of horsemen, the gray light glinting on shield rim and spear blade. They wore cloaks of the skins of horses, of cows and bears, with the head left on for a cowl so that they looked like the animals they had killed to clothe themselves.

"They are of Conchobor's court. They have hunted all day, and well," said Cathbad.

Nearer they came, the snow splashing like surf from the hooves of the horses, the air about them clouded thick with the breath of men and beast. They rode straight up and past us at a lumbering trot, so close I could hear the wheezing breathing of the tired horses. Across the fore- and hindquarters of their mounts, which were hung with necklaces of gold spheres and had headstalls richly decorated with stones, and snaffles of polished bronze, were the carcasses of the beasts they had killed.

A wild boar, its throat cut, its mouth agape, bloodied the hindquarters of one horse. Another had slung across it the forepart of a red deer, the antlers like a tree behind the rider; the thongs which held the corpse tight were black with frozen gore. The stiff bodies of geese dangled from many a horse. The men were silent, only grunting against the cold and the exertion of the ride.

They rode bareback, urging their mounts on with a tap on the neck from the haft of a spear.

"Where are they going?" I asked.

"To a false birth," said Cathbad. "We will go too."

Conchobor, now a full-grown man, himself was ahead, his great sword slung across his back. It was he who had killed the boar. Behind was Bricriu of the Poisoned Tongue. Cathbad named them for me. Bricriu's face beneath its cowl of animal skin was white as a sea pebble. The sun would not darken it, nor the wind either. His eyes, I knew, were green—a serpent in his ancestry.

"You will not have the Champion's Portion tonight, killer of two rabbits and a duck," Bricriu said, turning to me. I found I also was mounted, and that was what lay before me on the shoulders of my horse—two rabbits and a duck. As for Bricriu, he carried the hindquarters of a boar as his share of the chase.

"Perhaps you will be allowed the rabbit's balls in a little warm beer," Bricriu added, thrusting his white face close to mine.

"Perhaps it will be your guts I will use to give the beer flavor," I said, for I hated him.

"There is a house ahead," said Cathbad, uninterested in this encounter. "Let Bricriu ride forward and find out what shelter we may have there."

"Let Conall Cernach go with him," said Conchobor. "Bricriu to see but hold his poisoned tongue. Conall to speak." Conall Cernach was the son of Golden Head, who was the foster sister of Conchobor. Who was the father? That had never been decided. The two plunged off, the snow flying from the hooves of their horses. They were soon back; Conall said it was a small house and a poor one but they might all get into it, and the horses could stay in the lee of the house beside the dunghill, which was as tall as the roof.

"If they have beer, we have food," said Conchobor with a laugh.

We all jostled our way in and found the storeroom. There were two vats of beer in it, and five big jars of wine. The boar was skinned and butchered by torchlight in the snow—white snow, red blood and orange light. The hindquarters of the deer were flayed and cut into joints and all were quickly bubbling in a caldron over a great fire of turf.

"There must be a woman somewhere," said Conchobor, for the beer had aroused him and he was always full of lust. "Where is the woman of this house?"

((37))

"Bad luck that she can be no use to you," said her husband. "She is in labor at this moment."

"I will help her then," said Deichtine, sister to Conchobor. She got the name from the ten rings of red gold which she wore five on one arm and five on the other.

"Stay with me instead," said Conchobor. "If the woman is useless, you must do what you can."

Deichtine was not pretty, but well muscled, and fond of chariot-driving and hunting. "The child first," she said.

"That would be the best plan," said the husband. "It will not be long coming. There is a mare in the stable due to foal also. I will attend to the mare and the noble lady to my wife."

Some of the men, a little drunk, gathered around to watch the birth of the foal. Some held torches to watch the birth of the child.

"What omens, Cathbad?" they said. "Here are twice ten sires at this birth."

"Ten thousand and more split skulls," said Cathbad.

"A boy then," the men shouted, and thumped each other with their ringed fists.

The woman ignored the tumult but, gray-faced, her tunic hitched up around her breasts, squatted and grunted in labor in a corner of the room. Twice she screamed, and the scream had the sound of a hunting hound in it.

"He's here," cried Deichtine, for she had deftly received the boy's head in her hands, thrust between the woman's thighs. She held the baby up. "I love him as if he were my own," she cried, her face bloody from kissing him and biting the cord, which Cathbad gravely tied.

"He is yours then," cried Conchobor. "Come over to the fire now."

"First let me wipe off the baby and give him to the mother. Look what a man he is," she added, tickling the tiny genitals with her forefingers.

"I've better here and of more use," grumbled Conchobor. "Bricriu, take the flesh fork and give me some of the boar. A pity we did not roast him whole."

"I will roast you the biggest boar in Ulster," said Bricriu. "All shall come to the feast."

"Two foals from the mare," came a shout from the door. The husband and two warriors staggered in carrying the foals, their legs as long and straggly as wolfhounds. One was white and the other was gray.

Conchobor looked at them woozily. "Give them to the boy," he ordered. "What's born with him belongs with him. How is the woman now?"

"She is asleep," said Deichtine. "What will I call the boy?"

"Ask Cathbad."

Cathbad stood near me by the door, for the heat from the fire was now more than could be borne. Ice on one side. Fire on the other. The baby yelped like a dog and the men looked uneasily at each other. Bricriu sidled over and asked me with a sneer whether I wanted the rabbit's balls in my beer. The blow I gave him broke his nose. It also cut my knuckles to the bone; a small thing for such a pleasure.

"More room for swords outside," said Bricriu, wiping the spattered blood off his mouth with the back of his hand.

"Granted," said I, and stepped through the door into the darkness.

All disappeared—house, fire, caldron, dunghill, warriors, baby and foals. A lone presence beside me was an unlighted telephone booth. The wind howled up from the river. A taxi picked its way cautiously through the snow. I gave the driver my address and on the way asked him the time.

"Seven," he said, and added, "I'm on my way to the garage. Off in half an hour."

It was then only two hours since I had given Circe an *A* for her English paper. Provided it was the same day.

((39))

CHAPTER

4

I HAD NO LECTURE SCHEDULE THE NEXT DAY, BUT INSTEAD two hours of conferences with my students. That was in the afternoon. They came by individual appointment. Those two hours were a complete loss to me. Eighteenth-century England was utterly subdued by Bronze Age Ireland. Goldsmith and Gray, Johnson, Addison, Swift and Steele could not compare with those figures I had seen struggling through the snow on blown horses to that overcrowded house where the baby was born, and the two foals. The literary giants became ghosts. Conchobor and Cathbad, Conall Cernach and Bricriu became real.

I could not talk with conviction of Pope and the heroic couplet with the stench of beer, of wet hides, of mud and sweat in my nostrils. I struggled through the conferences bemused, and did little good for my students, who could not but be conscious of my state. One asked me whether I had flu, and another ventured to suggest massive doses of Vitamin C.

When they were all done—the interviews—I determined to walk to the tenement on Eighty-sixth Street. The snow had stopped falling some time during the night. The weather had in fact turned a little warm. Little snow remained around, except in the lee of window ledges and under gutterings. There was no wind. A stillness held the city, a stillness which seemed to mute the surge and ebb of the traffic.

I walked down Broadway to West Eighty-sixth Street, nervous and full of foreboding. I turned the corner of West Eighty-sixth Street, my heart beating with tremendous strokes and my mouth dry. The tenement was gone. In its place were a number of shops with offices or apartments over them. I walked all the way up one side of the street and down the other, as far as the park and back to Broadway, searching for the tenement. I found several, but all were occupied and certainly none was the place in which I had met Cathbad the Druid. I went home then, feeling as a man does who has been very drunk and has suffered a memory lapse concerning the scene of his drunkenness.

The Feast of Samhain, the Celtic feast which marks the merging of the worlds of the living and of the dead, survives in the Saxon All Hallow's E'en. It is the time of No-World—neither the world of the Quick nor that of the Dead. It was on the Feast of Samhain that I had found the tenement. It was mid-December before I found Circe again, waiting for me in my office at the end of the day.

She was as lovely as ever, blue jeans and all, as provocative, as mocking, as understanding, as desirable. My guts turned to water and my throat pounded at the sight of her. I wanted to be sick through sheer longing.

> *"No, Circe," cried Ulysses. "Never again.*
> *You have put an enchantment over me.*
> *Locked me in a cage. Despite all your promises*
> *You have turned me into that which I am not.*
> *And now I cannot escape your spell.*
> *Surely one of the gods will look at me with pity*
> *Who have come so far to face only*
> *. . . Madness."*

She kissed me on the end of the nose.

"Thanks for the *A*," she said. "Was I really that good?"

"Yes," I replied. "You were the unsuspected joy that lights the darkest corner of outermost space. Now catch your train to the Bronx."

"I don't have to go to the Bronx tonight," she said. "I'm coming home with you. I bought brown bread, red wine, cheese and liverwurst."

"My place is a mess," I replied. I thought of the moldering brown carpet, the piles of laundry in the bathroom, and the tiny living room all covered with books and records. I thought of the broken-down couch—it had been broken down when I bought it—and my bed, whose blankets had not been sent to the cleaners for months nor the linen changed in ten days—maybe two weeks.

"I stopped at Bloomingdale's and bought some sheets," she said. "They're a sort of a pale blue but they have small yellow roses on them."

"Fine," I said—surely the most inadequate reply ever made in such circumstances.

When we got to my place she started to clear up the mess. No questions about "Where does this go?" or "What shall I do with this?" She just cleared it up. Soon we were able to sit on the floor by an old walnut coffeetable I had bought somewhere and which was scored with cigarette burns and the rings of innumerable glasses.

She handed me a glass of red wine.

"You are on a long journey," she said simply.

"From Troy," I replied to go along with the joke. "I seek my home in Ithaka. It is so very far. I have angered the gods and been beset by misfortune and thrust into a blind alley in time.

"Polyphemos the Cyclops, the one-eyed monster son of Poseidon, devoured many of my men in his cave stinking with the droppings of monstrous sheep . . ."

"I don't like television myself," she said. "It's a bore." She popped a fragment of cheese into her mouth.

I ignored her. "I was given by a benefactor, none other than the great-hearted Aeolos himself, all the tempests and hurricanes of the world in a bag. I had but to keep them stoppered up,

> *and with a kindly wind straight from the*
> *blue and soothing southland,*
> *steer safely home over seas tinkling sweetly*
> *beneath the black sleek hull. . . ."*

"That thing with the man in the raincoat is not so bad," she said.

"Alas," I continued, "not trusting my men, I alone tended the tiller and sheet for nine days, so anxious was I to reach Ithaka and Penelope. But on the tenth day I grew weary and slept. My men released the winds and we were blown back all that distance we had sailed and, coming to an island of monsters, many of them were smashed to pulp by monstrous beings and eaten raw before my eyes, their flesh still quivering."

"Do you have 'Band on the Run'—The Wings?" she asked, turning over my mounds of records.

"You know nothing of Ulysses?"

She gave me a look thousands of years old.

"I like to do it with music," she said. Enchantresses speak directly of their desires.

Alas—The Wings, whoever they might be, had never dipped their oars in my wine-dark sea. We settled for "Clair de Lune," arranged for string quartet by a friend in the music department and played by a student quartet.

"What does it mean?" she asked, pushing the coffeetable aside and stretching out on the floor.

"Moonlight."

"Do it slowly," she said.

I settled beside her and dared to reach out and touch her hand, fingertip to fingertip. The intimacy of that touch made my whole body warm. Our fingers were entwined. We drew closer and I kissed her neck and felt her breath in my ear. I kissed her lips then, only slightly parted at first, but moist and soft. They opened and our tongues touched, as timorous as our fingertips. I rolled her on top of me and pulled her to my chest. Her hair fell past my face to the floor and was a cave to our lovemaking. Her body was as stiff and taut against me as a bowstave.

"God," I said, "I love you. I will never love life itself more than you in this moment."

If I could have I would have taken her within myself, filled some empty, lonely, unfillable yearning that lay there and that she now filled as if I had found at last what was missing of myself.

"Let's take off our clothes," she murmured.

She was much more graceful at undressing than I. Soon we were free of all garments and she was kneeling astride of me, her breasts full and perfectly formed, her waist small and my erection just touching the mound of her vulva. My knees were drawn up and her buttocks rested, white as marble, warm against my thighs.

"Slowly," she said. "Very slowly."

Her hips began to roll and her movements became longer and quicker, and I, falling into this rhythm, thrust and thrust again, slowly at first and then quicker and quicker until in ecstasy and pain the hot life jetted from me into her and we lay panting together.

"You're marvelous," she whispered. "Don't move. I like to feel him grow small and then big again. What are you thinking?"

"I'm composing a poem."

"Do you write poetry—not just teach it?"

"Yes. But it's difficult in these circumstances."

"Say a poem," she demanded.

"You have to understand something about poetry," I replied. "Poetry isn't just words. It's feelings. The nearer to the truth the feelings are, the greater the poetry. Everybody is a poet. Everybody feels truth even for the briefest moment, in the course of their lives."

She moved her hips a little more and repeated, "Say a poem."

I tried.

> *Love cries to love across the dust-dead years*
> *Across the barren waste of centuries, to lives*
> *Long lost, destroyed, thrown carelessly away,*
> *Unmarked and unremembered, Love calls.*
> *The maggot-ridden corpse, one week from breath*
> *The yellowed bones crushed in some ancient grave*
> *Touch fingertip to fingertip, breast to breast.*
> *Nor all black space nor flight of time*
> *Can silence the insistence of that call.*

"You're beautiful," she said. "You lie on me now, but do not move."

It was impossible not to move. Her eyes were dark as olives; her oval face, grave and almost sad. Her lips were slightly parted and I leaned up to kiss them.

"Two poems," she whispered. "The last one was the best."

We remembered the sheets from Bloomingdale's then, but we ate some more first—examining little details of our bodies and talking about each other the while.

She had had, I found, so ordinary an education that I cannot remember the details. She had learned something about reading in grade school and high school. She had, however, learned a great deal about boys and this was the subject which she most enjoyed.

"We exercised naked at school together," she said. "It was great fun."

"You went to an advanced school?"

The question puzzled her. "No. It was in the gymnasium that we exercised naked together. Isn't that the way everybody exercises at school?"

No, I thought. Not since Sparta fell—or at least not since the old gods were abolished and the New One, whose appalling sex-starved prophet was Paul, drowned out ecstasy.

"Let's bathe," she said. "I'll scrub you."

My bathroom was of the kind that has a tub instead of just a shower in a stall. She filled the tub with water and put in some pale green stuff out of a bottle with the scent of jasmine.

She filled it waist deep and poured
On joints unused to any but my own caress
Sweet unguents that soothed away each ache and strain.
Such balm makes pain a boon. Then drying me
She made each part her own,
Led me to the bed and soon was there herself.

"My name is Ulysses," I said. "It's the name of all men. We journey from a far land where in our youth we fought a hard and passionate war. Troy fell and many fell with Troy. We who are left are on our way home to Ithaka. We are old, but we must keep up the schemes and stratagems of the young or we will never complete our voyage. We must meet buckler to buckler, sword to sword, wit against wit, cunning against cunning. I cannot count the number of my comrades who are lost. I do not know how many may yet fall—myself among them perhaps. But always the dry stone crags and mountains of Ithaka call—the knifing winds and overpowering sun, the murmuring of the sea whose glittering waves glide upward among the tinkling pebbles of the beach. Always Ithaka—and Penelope. Will I know her? Will she remember me?"

She pressed her mouth against mine and ran her fingers through my hair.

"Show me out of pity the way to Hades which I must first visit so I may learn my fate," I said.

"You shouldn't drink so much wine," she replied. "You will have bad dreams."

We lay, her curve within my curve, and fell asleep at last.

CHAPTER

5

---

tHERE WAS A PALACE STANDING BEFORE A THRONG OF jolting, flying, earth-churning war chariots—a palace enclosed in outer walls of granite, glistening in the frosty air. Two gates of bronze, hanging on hinges thicker than the shafts of war axes, gave entrance. On one gate was a grinning face, the grin stretching from thick ear to thick ear.

"Salute Dagda the Fool, Father of All," said Cathbad, who was in a chariot with me.

On the other gate was the seated figure of a man, crudely done, with the antlers of a deer on his head and draped around his neck a serpent with the head of a ram.

"Cernunnos," said Cathbad. "He gives fertility to the earth."

Before the gate Conall Cernach, arriving first, raised a hunting horn to his lips and blew a shrill blast. Conchobor, not to be outdone, beat upon his shield with the flat of a small sword. The shield was called Ochain, meaning the Ear of Beauty, for it had four gold borders around it and a boss of ebony. It gave out a resounding ring. Flidais, who had but half a nose and was clad in horse leather to his calves, the blackened hide studded with nailheads of silver, raked his sword across the bars of the gate, making a high metallic clatter. His sword also had a name—Ochnech, the Cause of Sorrow. The others milled around in their chariots waiting for the opening of the gates—Sencha Mac Ailella, The Old One Full of Victories; Bricriu of the Poisoned Tongue; and Cor, Son of Cor.

I knew the fortress. It was that of Chulainn the Smith. Chained to the wall beside the gates by five chains, each attached to an iron collar about its neck, was a huge mastiff which plunged and bayed, teeth bared, at the men and horses. The brute was almost as big as a bear, its eyes red with madness.

"The hound of Chulainn," said Cathbad. "Only the Smith himself can approach it. There is neither man nor beast in all Ireland a match for that hound."

Aroused by the clamor of the weapons and the baying of the great insane dog, the gatekeepers came running to fling the gates open. Wheel to rocking wheel the chariots poured into the courtyard, the bronze rims raising thunder from the frozen cobbles.

Chulainn stood at the top of a flight of steps of green marble, before the massive doors of his palace, which were painted bright red, to welcome his guests. He was clad in a surcoat of gold cloth, for there was no wealthier man than he in all Ireland, since he was the master Smith of the Celts.

There was nothing he could not both design and fashion, in bronze, in silver or in gold. He alone of all the smiths in Ireland was fit to entertain kings such as Conchobor, and even kings from the Celts beyond the seas came to visit him. He had made two long-necked golden dogs for a Pharaoh's tomb, such was his fame, and around his thick hips he wore a marvelous sword belt of which I had previous knowledge, for it was the same belt that Herakles had worn.

> *Envy of that belt caused skin to crawl*
> *About my neck like exploring flies.*
> *Massy it was, and deeply carved*
> *With fanged leaping lion, boar and bear.*
> *Battle, slaughter and bloody death—all*
> *Lived within the circle of that belt. . . .*

When the chariots and horses had rattled away and all had entered the great hall of Chulainn—there were two score of warriors, of whom I have named but a few, together with their women—the Smith handed Conchobor a golden chalice set with emeralds and amethysts, brimming with purple wine, and said, "Drink deep—but tell me first, are all who accompany you now within the gates?"

Conchobor was not the man to answer such a question, but Cathbad answered for him. "All are here," he said. "None lagged behind. All arrived at once."

"Good," said Chulainn. "Soon we will be feasting and making merry. Such a palace as this needs a strong guard who will not be overcome by wine. That is the reason for my hound. If all are within, I will unleash him. The hound will be our safety from attack."

"Unleash him," said Conchobor, looking over the chalice at the women. "Unleash him and bring out your brimming vats and caldrons of boiled flesh."

"You are sure no one else comes?" said Chulainn. "That hound unleashed kills warriors as a cat kills mice—first biting off their heads."

"All are here," said Conchobor. "Unleash the hound and let us start the feasting."

Soon they were all seated at a table that stretched from one end of the hall to the other. Each kept his weapon by him, and swords, shields, javelins and sweating faces gleamed in the writhing flames of a hundred torches thrust into cressets in the walls. The feasting hall of Chulainn was so large that its roof was supported by fifty pillars, each clad in gold. The doors to the hall were also gold-clad, and of such size that mounted warriors passing through in a troop looked like a scattering of mice.

The best of the men of the kingdoms of Ulster and of Connaught were at Chulainn's feast, for there was peace for the time being between the two kingdoms. Cathbad named them for me—Furbaide with his red-gold shield, Orderg, glittering in the torchlight across his back; Cuscraid, whose great sword was called Coscrach, the Slaughterer, and was leaned, hilt up and ready for use, against the edge of the table beside him. Also Condere of the Great Shoulders, who, said Cathbad, had lifted a young bull and carried it, running, across a field. Far from us, his black-bearded split face in a heavy scowl, sat Fergus. He had reason for his ill humor, for he was the former King of Ulster, whose kingdom had been taken from him by Nessa, the White Mare, by a trick. The end of that story I got later.

When all were seated at the board, a whole roasted boar was brought in on a trencher carried by four men. All rose to get a glimpse of it, some standing on the table for a better view. It was laid on a table set before Conchobor, who was seated at the far end of the hall. The roasted skin gleamed bronze and shone with glistening fat. The mighty tusks curled up from the still-snarling jaws, and the deep-set eyes, replaced now with rubies provided by Chulainn, glared with hate at the assembly.

"Who carves the Champion's Portion?" roared Conchobor, standing over the boar. "Let each make his boast."

"Who but Conall Cernach?" asked Bricriu of the Poison Tongue, looking slyly at Cor, son of Cor, who was opposite him. "No one but he deserves the honor. Not a night has passed since he took arms, but he has slept with the head of an enemy under his knee."

"No champion he," cried Cor, flushing with anger. "One such head had never been shaved, and was that of a boy new to arms."

"You shame yourself, so fine a warrior, with such slanderous talk," said Conall. "It's because that head was the head of your son that you speak in this unseemly way, without thought or at least without having inquired what is the truth. The boy challenged in the dark, demanding combat, and I killed him, not knowing his age."

"No shame on you then," said Cor, son of Cor. "No need for a warrior such as you to tell lies before this host."

"That is true," said Conall.

"Nevertheless," said Bricriu softly, "surely a tried warrior, after a few blows are struck, would know whether he fought a man or a boy. No boy fights like a seasoned warrior."

Lamthapad, the Swift to Hand, Conall's sword, arced across the hall and embedded itself in a golden pillar close to Bricriu's pale face.

"Was that a champion's feat?" asked Conall softly.

"It was," said Bricriu.

"Do you wish combat?"

"I do not."

"Then silence your tongue or lose your head," said Conall and, moving from his place, pulled the sword out of the pillar. When he had it free he gave it a flick and a tuft of Bricriu's beard fell down his chest to the table.

"It would be safer for you, Bricriu, mixing among men, if you shaved," said Conall, and returned to his place.

"Come," cried Conchobor, "the boar grows cold. Who challenges Conall for the Champion's Portion? Is it agreed that it is his?"

Many challenged, emboldened by wine and the heft of their bright swords.

"The portion should be mine," said Flidais. "Five men of Connaught I gutted in one hour at the Ford of the Fairing."

"An Ulster trick," said a Connaught man. "You Ulster warriors know the potholes and back men into them and bring them down. It is no braver than killing fish."

"Your head on my belt at the close of the feasting," said Flidais.

"Not so," said the Connaught man. "Yours rather to match your brother's. A loving pair." He reached inside his surcoat of leather and pulled out a severed head, which he flung at Flidais. It hit him full in the face, breaking his nose and splitting his lips. The head tumbled on the floor among the rushes beside Flidais. He picked it up. It was the head of his brother.

Little notice was taken of that beyond a laugh from the others. But the boasting was not over, and swords were picked up and bucklers slipped onto shield arms. To avoid a massacre Conchobor made his judgment.

"The Champion's Portion belongs to Conall Cernach," he said. "The matter is settled."

Settled it might have been but for Dubthach, the Dark One. He was seated opposite me and, with eyes glittering with malice, he said, "It is but courtesy that we inquire whether this new warrior who comes from far-off Greece and who at our last meeting contributed two rabbits and a duck to the spoils of the chase wishes to make his boast or prefers to remain in prudent silence."

"Make your claim then," said Conchobor, "you who have fought as you say in wars of which we have never heard. Or perhaps you think, knowing truthfully your own deeds, that Conall should be declared the greatest among us."

A hand reached out, dipping into a great bowl of wine with a ladle. The wine lapped against the sides of the bowl as the sea against rocks. I heard again the groan and thump of the long oars against the thole pins, and the grunt of the oarsmen pulling against the set of the wine-dark sea.

The challenge could not be ignored.

"Little as I know of the deeds of Conall Cernach," I replied, "I do not decry them. He seems a splendid fighting man. Surely I would have welcomed that swift strong arm of his at the walls of Troy. Certainly he would have leaped out of the horse's belly at the moment for slaughter and been first among the Trojan spears. Yet he was not there, though I was there myself, a leader of the host that slew their thousands. Great as are the feats of Conall Cernach they cannot match mine, nor those of the least of the men of Ithaka who accompanied me to Troy. Except perhaps that poor fellow, tried but a few years in arms, who fell off the roof of the house of the enchantress Circe when drunk, and so broke his neck. Yes, perhaps Conall Cernach might well have overmatched him. But to those others of us returning from Troy, chief among them myself, I say he must take second place.

"Not merely in the war in which he took no part does he lack deeds of manly valor," I continued, "but can he boast of days of combat with those white horses that rule the seas at the bidding of Poseidon, charging line upon line, thundering in their fury, upon our frail black craft to batter it under their hooves? Or has he, with a burning brand, put out the eye of the Cyclops, son of Poseidon, or fought flesh-eating monsters, their jaws dribbling with the blood of his comrades, or overcome goddesses who turned all his comrades into grunting swine and snuffing bears?

"Can Conall Cernach match these boasts? If not, let him move away from the boar while I carve for myself the Champion's Portion."

"I will not cede to you, stranger called Uliseacht," cried Conall the Victorious. "However, if you will try with javelin or sword, ax or hammer, all may soon be decided."

Then Conall, wily and experienced warrior that he was, without another word flung his blood-seeking javelin at me. So quick and strong his hand, the javelin would have pierced my eye had I not, battle trained, quickly moved aside. Then he rushed at me and made the shield stroke—a cunning blow, but one which I avoided, expecting it. It was well done—no doubt of that—the razor-sharp shield edge sweeping like a blade level with my neck.

I leaped up onto the table and smashed my own shield edge into Conall's upturned face. Back he toppled, head bent, and I drove my sword at his belly. The point entered before he pulled aside. But at that moment there came from beyond the great gold doors the raging bark of the mad hound of Chulainn, sharp with murder. The sound silenced the tumult in the hall and stopped our combat. Men seized their weapons and the women cowered to the walls. Sweet the taste of their tender throats and entrails if that mad creature should break through the door.

"Do not be afraid," shouted Chulainn. "Some stranger has approached unbidden in the dark, or a group of robbers have attempted to scale the walls. Alas for them. In the morning we will find but a smear of blood here and there—a little dock leaf perhaps or a tuft of grass splashed with gore. But nothing more. Not even a bone."

Conall reached for his sword, which he had dropped, and I brought my own down on his skull; the blood drowned his face. Suddenly the savage, strident barking ended, as if choked off by an iron hand. Then came three blows against the golden doors, which at a signal from Chulainn were opened cautiously by his men. In came a boy, tall, broad-shouldered and golden-haired. He wore the short tunic of a youth who has not yet taken arms, and carried in one hand a ball and in the other a curved stick for hitting it with in the game known among the Celts as hurley. He looked about at the company, flung the ball left-handed down the hall and right-handed flung the stick after it—with such skill that the curved stick hit the ball and drove it upward against the ceiling.

"Where is my hound?" cried Chulainn. "Why is he silent?"

"I killed him," said the boy. "He came at me out of the darkness, his red eyes like fire. I flung the ball down his maw, seized him by the hind legs and battered his brains out against the wall." He looked fearlessly at Chulainn. "You should set a better guard than that for your feasting," he said.

"Who is this who has killed the best watchdog in Ulster?" demanded Chulainn.

"It is the boy Sétanta," said Conchobor. "I had forgotten that I said he could follow us."

"What kind of boy is it that kills such a hound?" demanded the Smith. "Who is his father? To whom was he given in fosterage?"

"As to who his father is, that is uncertain," said Conchobor. "But I will tell you his story. The last time we saw the stranger Uliseacht (who must certainly now be awarded the right to carve the Champion's Portion) we were hunting and stopped in the snow at night at the house of a man whose wife was in labor. A boy was born to the woman, and my sister of the Ten Gold Rings adopted the boy. We were far from my palace and next day had to drive through heavy snow, and the boy did not survive the journey.

"My sister grieved so much over the boy's death that nothing could be done to comfort her. However, all her wailing made her thirsty, and she was given a goblet of wine. When she had sipped the wine she said immediately that she had swallowed some live creature which had entered her belly and made her pregnant."

"That is because you slept with your sister the night before when the boy that died was born," said Dubthach. "You impregnated her."

"It is true that I slept with her, but Cathbad said that the creature in the wine was the spirit of the boy for whom my sister was grieving," said Conchobor. "Besides," he added, "I was not the only one who slept with my sister that night. The point is that she was pregnant from the moment she drank the wine, and as her belly swelled it was necessary to find her a husband, for a fatherless boy has no heritage. So it was agreed to marry her to Sualdam Mac Roich. But she was ashamed to go to bed with her swollen belly on her wedding night and so circled the bed to the right to bring good luck to it. As she completed the circle she said that whatever she had in her womb slipped from her. Later, however, she gave birth to this boy, and while he is certainly the son of my sister Deichtine, whether he is some magical creature which slipped into my sister while she was drinking wine, or whether he is my son or even perhaps the son of Dubthach, or some other, no man, not even Cathbad, can say. Now let Uliseacht carve the Champion's Portion, as is his due, and the boy may dine with us."

"I cannot sit to eat at the table of a man I have robbed, even to save my life," said the boy.

"That is easily remedied," said Chulainn. "Since you have killed my watchhound, you must replace him until you find or train one as good."

"Agreed," said the boy. "I will be your hound until I can provide another. Do not worry. No one will get by me."

"If you are my hound you must have a new name," said the Smith. "From now on you will be called the Hound of Chulainn—Cúchulainn."

"Agreed," said the boy.

"Carve the boar," said Conchobor to me, and I drew my sword to cut the Champion's Portion from the nape of the neck.

"One moment," said Cathbad, stopping me. "Listen, Conchobor and all here, to what I say. Mark each word. Let no details escape your mind."

A mist arose around him, streaming through the rush-covered stones of the floor. All stared, for this was the seer's mist, and hands moved to eagles' claws, polished bones and other amulets which guard against the spirit world. Out of the seer's mist came Cathbad's voice, saying:

No Hound of Chulainn alone
Is this golden boy.
Skull breaker,
Spine cleaver,
Chariot warrior;
The shriek of Death,
Such is he.

A feeder of vultures
And carrion crows.
He will feast them
On the bowels of warriors.
None will bring him down
But the leg of a dog.
Your warriors will turn
To women, O Conchobor.
Then Cúchulainn alone
Will guard the road
To Royal Ulster.

The seer's mist was gone. There was silence in the great hall at that prophecy, except for the crackle of the fire and the sputtering of the torches.

CHAPTER

6

GREAT FAIR WAS BEING GIVEN AT THE PALACE OF Conchobor. There were races of every kind, and weapon contests, and feasting, singing and storytelling.

Cattle herds from every part of Ireland were brought to the fair. From Ath Luain came four thousand head, brown, some speckled, full uddered, small footed. From the Stone of Granaird came six thousand, black and rough coated, their nostrils streaming snot, for they had been driven hard. High priced they were, for black cows give whitest milk.

From Irain came two thousand, gray-and-white of Gaulish breed, and from Smirohmaith, six thousand of the small close-haired kind. These live on poorest grass. Their hides are as good as horse for shield coverings and warriors' coats.

The cattle were all penned in great folds to the west of Conchobor's palaces. He had three of them at that time. The first was called Craebruad, the Red Branch, and here lived Conchobor himself and the two thousand warriors. The second was called Tete Brec—that is, the Spotted or Twinkling House. Here were kept all the jeweled swords and spears and shields and war gear, the horse jewelry and golden armor with silver inlays that belonged to Conchobor. The third was called Craederg, the Gory Branch. Here were kept, each in its proper niche, the heads of warriors who had fallen to the swords, spears and battle axes of the men of Ulster. Also their slings and shields. There were many of them, each well known. The heads of the most famous rested on pillars, their hair combed and their beards dressed. Cathbad took me there. He spoke to them and they answered him civilly but in dreamy voices. Some, very long dead, answered only in a whisper.

There was one post without a head.

"For what noble personage is that pillar reserved?" I asked.

"It is not yet known," said Cathbad. "For one of two people."

"Well, who are they?"

"Yourself or Bricriu."

"When will this matter be decided?"

It was the gray head of Macmantir na Cruach that answered me in ghostly whisper.

"A fool's question," he said. "Why throw the shadow of death into golden life? You live now. That is sufficient."

A great number of splendidly glazed pots occupied niches near each head.

"They are the brains of the warriors," said Cathbad. "Your own might be preserved here if thought worthy." He took the lid off a pot and handed me such a brain. It was much shrunken—hardly the size of a ball—and red in color, having been mixed with earth to preserve it.

"Let us go to the fair," now said Cathbad. "It was Conchobor who planned it. Little good will he get from it—indeed he was well named. Conchobor the Fool."

"He seems wise and warriorlike," I said.

"In all the world there is to be only one truly wise man. Nor will he be a warrior. He will be put to death by torture."

"Why such a death for a worthy man, though not a man of weapons?"

"Because wisdom is a pain to the unwise. The greatest wisdom is the greatest pain, and they will not endure it." He looked closely at me from those near-set eyes which seemed to pinch his long nose together. "You have a little wisdom, Uliseacht. For that reason I sought you out. But too much learning makes a fool of you. Learn to live as you once lived; not to study books and take dry script for flowing wine and blood."

We left the Craederg, having first taken respectful leave of all the revered and noble heads of the slain warriors. That empty pillar, as I passed it, caused me to shudder. Cathbad saw the shudder. "Since all must die, surely it cannot be death that you fear. Perhaps what you fear is that you have not lived. Tomb-sealed from your first breath. That is a terrible fate. You owe three heads to her who delivered you."

"You know of her?"

"I know all except what the gods have reserved to themselves."

Outside, the bawling and moaning of the cattle filled the air, with behind it the harsh cawing of crows which gathered to feed on their fodder. The smell of the urine of the cattle reached even the central hall of Conchobor's palace. There great vats of wine from the Helvetii were being traded for bulls, cows, shields, swords and sword belts.

The pens for the cattle had been built on a hill to the west of the three palaces so that Conchobor and those with him could enjoy the strong and heartwarming smell. The cattle had fed on their way to the fair on the green grass of Ireland, which was at its lushest. Their dung flowed in rivers from the hills on which they were penned. In places it was necessary to wade calf deep through their ordure. This strengthens the feet, and gives a good flow of blood through the body. Some drove chariots through these pools of liquid dung to strengthen the wheels. The charioteers, whenever they splashed someone in this way, called out, "Long life to you."

It was a merry fair. Such fairs we had also in Ithaka. Besides the sale of cattle and slaves, and torques of gold and necklaces of jet and shields and swords and wine and warriors' cloaks and tunics and cloaks of silver thread for noble women, there were wrestling matches and displays of skill with the sling and spear and horse sword. Then a blast was blown on three trumpets. All was silent. The three silver apples which were carried over the head of Conchobor gave their tingling sound. The wind even stopped moving so all men might hear what was to be said by King Conchobor, the Great of Heart.

"A challenge," he cried, a little drunk. "I will race any moving thing in Ulster or Connaught or Leinster or Munster in my chariot, driving myself. I will race eagles or swallows or chariots or men on horseback or on foot, armed or naked, or whoever or whatever wishes to race against me."

"What course?" asked Conall Cernach, always ready.

"Thrice around the three castles," replied Conchobor. "Are you ready, Conall the Victorious? Celtar also, are your two black stallions yoked? Cormac—is it snails you have hitched to your war cart, or the steeds of a warrior?"

Such taunting was not to be resisted. Conall, Cormac, and Celtar leapt to their chariots.

"A moment while I grease the axle," cried Celtar, whose red beard had turned many a sword stroke aimed at his throat. He seized a small pig, cut its throat in a second and let the blood pump over the bearing of the chariot wheel. The wheel was of the finest alder wood, light, and in two pieces doweled together and with a rim of bronze.

Off they went. At the first circuit Celtar's wheel struck a

rock; he was thrown from his chariot and his head smashed.

"So much for grease," cried Cormac, jabbing his pointed goad into the flanks of his gray steeds. But luck was against him too. Indeed a raven had been seen sitting on the rim of his chariot the evening before. Down went one gray and over its head went Cormac, the chariot on top of him. Conchobor won.

Many others tried—in chariot and on horseback. But Conchobor could not be beaten.

Then a man came to the king who was very rich in land and cattle, though he was not a warrior. He was dressed in his best clothes—a cape of blue, a tunic of green and long breeches of white tied with black lacings in the Gaulish manner. His name was Crunniuc Mac Agnomain.

"I have a wife who is faster than your stallions," he said.

"Send for her," said Conchobor.

Heralds were sent to the house of the man. He lived in the mountains. His cattle were of the old kind that will thrive on wiry grass and even bog willow and sedges.

The heralds arrived and found the woman. "You are to race against the stallions of the king," one of them said.

"Some other time," said the woman. "I am close to labor. My child is due this very day."

"You will race now or be killed, and your child too," said the herald. "Conchobor does not wait on a woman's convenience. It is your husband's boasting that has brought this on you."

"The boast of the husband lifts the heart of the wife," said the woman, and went with them. She came to Conchobor.

"Who are you?" he asked, eyeing her bursting belly.

"I am Macha, the scald crow my totem, daughter of Sainrith Mac Imbaith. But I cannot run now, as you can see."

"Strip for the race," said Conchobor with a laugh.

The woman turned to the crowd around. "Every man among you and every woman among you and every child among you came from the womb," she said. "This day, perhaps this hour, I am to produce a child such as you. Is it fitting then that I should race stallions? Remembering your own mothers who gave you birth, have pity."

The men jeered. "A woman is certainly a useless being," they said. "Two or three days out of every month she flows thin blood and cannot have intercourse. Then, bearing a child, at the very time when she should be at her strongest, lion-like, filled with vigor and fury, she is at her weakest. This one can hardly walk unless you call that waddle of hers a walk. Let her run. Her big-mouthed husband should make good his boast."

"A boast unfulfilled stinks like rotten food," said Bricriu.

"If I run, I die," cried the woman. "My child too. Have pity on me."

"She should not run," said Cathbad. "I give you warning, Conchobor."

"What?" cried Conchobor in a fury. "Is a fat pig of a man who does not even fight, but only raises cattle, to make a public boast that his wife, pregnant, can outrun the king's stallions? Is that boast to be left unchallenged? Did I challenge her? Are people to whisper that Conchobor was afraid to race his fine horses against so weak a thing as a pregnant woman? Strip, woman, and prepare to race. It is your king's order."

"I give you solemn warning," said Cathbad.

> *Against nature*
> *No man should raise a hand,*
> *Nor interfere.*
> *Ruin comes from such pride.*
> *You fight birth itself,*
> *Conchobor the Fool.*
> *Your prize then,*
> *Sterility and Pain.*

"It is the foreign man beside him who has made Cathbad so

discourteous," said Bricriu. Quickly he flung a javelin at me. His was always the treacherous stroke. There was no time to do more than turn a shoulder. The javelin struck the rim of my shield, flew upward, the shield humming, turned and, descending, landed by chance in the body of the small pig whose throat Celtar had cut to grease the wheels of the chariot.

"A worthy target, Bricriu," I said and, taking up the javelin, flung it left-handed at him. It passed between his knees. "A warning, Bricriu," I said. "A warrior such as I could have thrown higher."

"Let us have the race," said the king.

The woman Macha stripped and looked at him with cold, glittering eyes. Her belly was firm, well muscled. Her buttocks were splendid, and her legs strong and long boned— the legs of a good runner.

"Put the goad to your stallions," she said.

Off they went then. At the end of the first circuit the woman screamed and gave birth to a son. At the end of the second circuit she screamed again and gave birth to a girl. Each scream terrified all who heard it. At the end of the third circuit she was two paces ahead of the stallions of Conchobor. She fell dead, all blood from her womb to her feet.

"Well, she beat me," said Conchobor.

"She has done more than beat you," said Cathbad. "She has destroyed your kingdom."

Conchobor looked around. "All seems well," he said. "I see no hosts approach. I hear no battle shouts or rumblings or chariot wheels or trumpets blown."

"She has conquered you in this manner," said Cathbad. "She has transferred to every warrior in Ulster the same labor pangs from which she suffered when you made her race. Remember in detail what I tell you now.

"For nine years to come, whenever Ulster is in peril, all her warriors who heard that woman scream, from the greatest to the least, will suffer the weakness and pangs of a woman in labor. They will suffer the pains of childbirth for four days and five nights or for five days and four nights, according to when the danger arrives. Your men will become women to you when you need them most, as I foretold."

"That is a hard penalty for losing a race," said Conchobor. "That wasn't in the bargain. However, what must be borne must be borne. Answer me this. After the birth pangs, will the men give birth to fine sons?"

"The question you ask was answered before," said Cathbad. "You were so full of pride in your stallions that you did not listen, when I said,

> *'You fight birth itself,*
> *Conchobor the Fool.*
> *Your prize then,*
> *Sterility and Pain.*
>
> *'Your warriors*
> *After labor*
> *Will give birth—*
> *To nothing.'* "

Conchobor turned to his sister, Finnceann the Golden-Headed, who had several children. She was so lusty that she had even taken Bricriu between her thighs.

"Are the pains of labor heavy?" he asked.

Finnceann smiled. "There's no greater pain known," she said. "But for women there is this consolation—first comes the delight of the strange and strong man touching her hair and eyes, kissing her lips and holding her in his strong arms. For you there will be no such consolation."

Ever afterward the place where Conchobor's palaces stood was called Emain Macha—that is to say, the place of the Twins of Macha, the Scald Crow.

Cúchulainn alone, of the hosts of Ulster, was not present at the fair to hear the screams of the woman.

CHAPTER

7

---

a FTER THE DEATH OF MACHA I SAID TO CATHBAD, "You are an illusion. I fell asleep in the arms of Circe and I dreamed of you."

"Circe is a magician?" asked Cathbad.

"She is at present a student at Columbia University in New York City, United States of America."

Then there came other images. I saw an island—a green springtime island like an emerald, triangular in shape, floating in a pale blue and utterly calm ocean. I saw the figure of blind Tiresias in the Land of Death, his golden staff glowing in the gloom, making his way toward the pool of blood which

I, Ulysses, guarded from the other dead, even my own mother, with my sword.

> *"Drink of the blood, noble prince of Thebes."*
> *That is what I said and, bending, he pursed*
> *His wan lips and sucked the dark gore thirstily*
> *And said, "If you, Ulysses, master of sea ways*
> *Would safely come to stony Ithaka*
> *Do not raid the cattle of the sun*
> *Grazing on the cool hills of Cuailnge. . . ."*

"Trinakria," I cried, but he was gone, and Cathbad stood before me.

"Soon I will wake up," I said.

"That feat has never yet been performed," he replied.

"You are talking nonsense."

"That feat has never yet been performed either," he reflected. "There is neither sense nor nonsense. There are neither dreams nor waking. All are one. Also each man lives every man's life. We are each other. Difference is a word of evil. It is the maggot that devours the fruit of life. . . ."

His voice drifted into silence. I felt cold. My left foot was cold and, indeed, the whole of my left side. I opened my eyes and saw the gray light of ghostly-fingered dawn drifting into my bedroom.

Circe had pulled the covers over herself and left me naked on the blue sheets with the little yellow roses. I was so glad to see her and to be away from Cathbad and that gory palace of Conchobor and the serpent eyes of Bricriu that I just reached out my hand to touch her lying there, beautiful as a solitary pearl.

But at last the cold was beyond endurance. It was plain I would have to wake her.

"Darling," I said.

She grunted—a little grunt of pure animal content. "Later," she said. "I'm sleepy."

"Darling," I repeated. "You've got all the blankets. I'm freezing to death."

The pains of men are of no concern to goddesses. She was lying with her back to me, so I reached beneath her dark hair and pulled a corner of the blanket over my shoulder. Grudgingly she rolled on her back and without opening her eyes said, "I love you."

I touched the tip of her ear with my finger. Surely nothing ever was so delicately or beautifully formed. "You don't really love me," I said. "You enjoy making love to me."

"I love you as pearls love candlelight," she said. "I love you as the ocean loves the west wind. I have loved you through eternity."

I kissed her. Later she said, "What dream did you have?"

I told her. She sat there, the blankets draped over her thighs, her elbows supported on her knees and her chin propped in her hands, and listened thoughtfully.

"You are the cause of this," I said. "It is only since I knew you that I have met Cathbad and he takes me back into that dim land and time."

"That wasn't the idea," she said. "I mean I really didn't know anything about Goldsmith and I just had to have a good grade on that paper."

My heart sank through a trillion miles of darkness. The blow to the human male when he finds that he is actually just another pickup is almost as great as the blow of death itself.

"But I really love you," she added. "Otherwise I wouldn't have let you into my pants. You see I had this Goldsmith thing —and I loved you as well. I used to look at you in class. Sometimes you weren't even there. I mean you were thousands of miles away—years too. Real gone. I wanted to be with you —wherever it was you were. Other guys, they're just—nothing."

"They're younger," I said. I was looking for any kind of balm to pour on the wound caused by Goldsmith—poor pocked Goldsmith whose only erotic outlet in all his life had been his fantasies and the whores of Dublin and London.

"That's nothing," she said almost contemptuously. "They don't really know how to do it. Before you know it they're shoving at you and you're not even ready. Just because they're ready they think that makes you ready. Besides. It's something else. Sort of magical. It's being filled with life in someone special's arms. I don't know how to say it."

"You felt that way about me?"

"Yes."

"Then I hope I don't wind up with my head on that pillar on Conchobor's Gory House."

"I won't let you," she said. "But maybe you ought to see a shrink. I went to one once. He did me some good."

"Why did you go?"

"I kept dreaming this dream."

"What dream?"

"Well, I'd meet all these great-looking guys—you know, like football players and baseball players and so on. And we'd have a big party and then I'd turn them all into animals. Wolves and lions and pigs. The funny thing was that I liked turning them into animals and yet I felt sorry for them."

"What did the psychiatrist say?"

"He asked me if anyone had ever tried to rape me or anything like that. He said I hated men. He ate mints all the time. I think he had a thing about whether his breath smelled. Watching those TV commercials."

"Did the dreams go away?"

"Sort of."

"What do you mean—sort of?"

"Well, after he'd said I hated men I got to thinking about it. I was a virgin then. So I tried one. It hurt. In fact it wasn't that hot. I was too scared anyway, and he had a dong like a baseball bat. And it was in the back seat of a Nova. But it wasn't that bad the second time and I found I didn't hate men. In fact, I liked them. Still do. But I didn't have those dreams anymore. Just other ones. I think dreams are interesting. There ought to be a book about them."

"There are—lots," I replied. "Look, in this dream about turning men into animals was there one man you couldn't turn into an animal?"

She thought about that question a long time. "No," she said.

"I hope you dream of him," I said. "Because unless you do and take pity on me, I am lost and can never reach Ithaka. The man's name is Ulysses."

"I used to know a basketball coach called Ulliman," she said. "He'd be as hot as a pistol and then he couldn't come. I gave up on him." She flung the blanket off and stepped naked out of the bed, utterly oblivious to the pieces of my ego and my love she had cut up and left writhing with her talk of the basketball coach.

"Where's the bathroom?" she asked. "I need a shower and I have to take a pee."

CHAPTER

8

CIRCE WENT AWAY AT CHRISTMAS TO HER FOLKS IN the Bronx, and I was very lonely. Forlorn is a better word. I decided I would have to endure the vacation day by grinding day, as a man endures a prison sentence. I mooned around the university library, rereading Irish mythology. It was curious. The findings of the archeologists, into which I also looked, seemed far less believable than the myths themselves.

Then it occurred to me that I had both the time and the money to go to Ireland, and I was seized with the compulsion to go and visit, not far from Dublin, the royal burial mound called New Grange of which I had read so much.

I went. I won't detail the journey except to say that during it I found that Cathbad was right about the intermixture of the real and the unreal, of past, present and future.

When the plane left Kennedy and reached its cruising altitude, Earth disappeared. Below—very far below—lay a field of clouds of continental extent, for it reached from the United States coastline all the way to Ireland. It was true, of course, that the clouds were but moisture which cut off the view of the world below. But if there are clouds of the air, may there not also be clouds of the mind? Was one of those clouds of the mind, I asked myself, the human conviction that we live in Time, and both Past and Future are beyond our reach and our view, whereas in actuality they are there, quite as real as the world itself below the obscuring meadows of cumulus? If we could penetrate the Time Cloud, might we not find perhaps a continuum hard to describe except in terms of a sphere which has no beginning and no ending unless an arbitrary line is drawn on it?

I rested for a day in Dublin, and then hired a car and drove up the Boyne valley to New Grange, where the royal graves dating from the Bronze Age were located. The place was closed down. I had not thought of it, but there were not enough tourists in winter to justify keeping the site open.

On one side of the road there was a tourist office (closed) and a curio and book shop (closed). On the other side, up a slight hill, seemingly in a farmer's rough pasture, lay the tumulus, a vast mound under which the graves lay.

Irritated, I walked toward the mound along a fence of slight iron railings. The mound, though huge, was somehow not as impressive as I had expected. It was just a hill of moderate size, and one is accustomed to seeing hills of moderate size. Two cows, browsing nearby in the winter-brown grass, examined me with indifference.

There were a number of huge stones before the entrance

to the passage in the mound leading to the graves within. Some of these were inscribed with spirals and others with lozenge shapes. When I saw the lozenge shapes I thought immediately of palm trees. They looked to me exactly the way a palm tree looks when frond after frond has been cut off the growing stem.

Once at Delos, near Apollo's shrine
I saw a young palm, lovely as a girl
So full of grace and stateliness
The tears burst from my eyes at the very sight.
My warriors wondered to see me so disturbed
Grizzled by battle with blows yet to come
By that young heart-raising tree. . . .

Looking at the carved stones I saw, for a moment, the palm at Delos, the arid dusty earth around, the verdant fronds green-gold with sunlight with here and there soft shadows like gentle fingers reaching down.

It was a cold day, the air thin and pinched. But this was Ireland, and in a moment the air grew magically warmer and rain started to fall—a soft, steady, mournful rain that made the huge stones glisten with liquid light. The rain formed rivulets which ran down the zigzag of the lozenge carvings. A gate of iron railing closed the entrance to that long passage which leads to the central burial chamber deep in the bowels of the mound. It was locked and unscalable.

Around me the landscape appeared and disappeared as seething walls of rain swept across the fields from the distant mountains. Here and there shafts of wan sunlight struck through the rain. All was held between light and dark. Out of the white rain a man walked toward me. He had a pipe in his mouth, the bowl turned down to keep the tobacco burning. He came through the wall of rain with slightly hunched shoulders and stopped before me.

" 'Tis shut for the winter," he said. "Are you come far?"

"New York."

With the rain dripping off the brim of his felt hat, he considered the problem. "If you'll go on to Knowth there's one there that's open. You have a car?" he said.

"Yes."

"I'd take you myself, but the cattle are in want of milking. You can't miss Knowth." With that he was gone.

I found the grave easily. There was no gate to bar the entrance. A shaft lined with worn steps brought you below the ground to the corridor of stones which led to the central burial chamber. Each stone was about six feet in height and perhaps two or three feet wide. The stones were set side by side. Roof stones of the same size lay across them, completing the passage.

It was the smell of the place and not its look that made it real. It stunk of cattle urine. The shaft leading to the passageway of stones was in a slight depression. The urine of the cows standing about in the pasture above was washed down into the grave by the rains. It was the stench I remembered, together with that of cattle dung, from Emain Macha on the day of Conchobor's fair—a stench so familiar it would rejoice the spirits of the dead kings.

With the rain hissing into the grass above I turned and moved up the ancient passage to the central burial chamber. The light from the entrance shaft dimmed as I walked uncertainly on. At one place the pillars of stone had leaned inward so that I was able to get between them sideways only. Indeed, for one terrible moment I felt myself caught, pinned spine and chest between those mighty boulders.

> *And then came shapes in thousands*
> *Rustlings and whisperings everywhere*
> *Movements of darkness and cold winds*
> *That turned my bones to ice.*

I moved on to the burial chamber and found the light

brighter. At first it was no more than a glimmering and then it grew brighter and warmer. Instead of the gray burial chamber with its dead stone bowl to hold cremated bones, I came to a large chamber. It was of stone indeed, but seemed newly built, with a passage leading off to one side. From this passage, into which the light did not penetrate, I heard deep, heavy breathing. It was the breathing of an animal, and an animal of great size. I heard the beast move toward me, the hooves clumping and the horns scraping against the walls. In that cold chamber I saw first its steamy breath come out of the passage ahead of it, and smelled the sweat from its hide. Then there stepped into the light a splendid bull, twice the size of any I had ever seen. It was white, the wide-set eyes red-rimmed with rage. The horns were vast sweeping curves, and ropy saliva streamed from its mouth. It stood twice as high as I when it entered the chamber and, head held high, looked at me.

Then it turned and moved off down the passage from which it had emerged.

CHAPTER

9

a T FIRST I WAS TREMENDOUSLY RELIEVED THAT THE bull had gone. Then, in the kind of fear which has a basis in curiosity, I followed it, wondering how it had got into the ancient grave shaft—for I still thought it a creature of the present time.

As it moved majestically off, the thought occurred that it was leading me somewhere. The muscles of its hindquarters rolled powerfully, and the sound of its hooves sent heavy echoes up the narrow passageway of crude and carved stones. It bellowed once—a terrifying sound that shook every stone of the passageway and every fiber of my body.

Then the bull turned abruptly down a side passage and stood there, blocking that particular alley. The main passage continued ahead; I went by cautiously and, after a few paces, climbed three great steps of stone to find myself in a sumptuous bedchamber, the floor covered with bearskins, the walls draped with shields and swords, the bed itself of ebony, richly decorated in inlaid silver and gold in patterns of animals and flowers with, in the center of the footboard, the head of a brood mare, exquisitely done.

In the bed lay a man and a woman—the woman red-haired, her cheekbones sharp, her eyes aslant, her lips red. Beside her the man slept, snoring.

"Medb is my name," said the woman as I entered. "This is Ailill, my mate—a lazy stallion for so brisk a mare." She eyed me and seemed pleased that I had come.

"Wake up," she said, poking the man with an elbow. "Wake up. I have something to say to you."

"I'm tired. Let me be," he replied.

"You said last night that it was a good thing to be the wife of a wealthy man," said the woman Medb. "That has vexed me all night. It is what I want to talk about. Do you think, for instance, that a wealthy man has a better manner of making love than a poor man? If that is the case let me assure you it is not so. We have few poorer in all Connaught than the pig-keeper, and when I lay with him, he was delicious."

"That is not what I meant," said Ailill, settling himself deeper into the pillow.

"Well, what did you mean? Come. I have a judge here who knows nothing of either of us. Say what you meant by vexing me so."

"I meant only that you are better off now than the day I married you, in wealth of every kind," said Ailill. "Now let me sleep. There can be no argument about that, and there is nothing in it to vex you."

"How can you make such a boast?" demanded Medb. "Surely your arrogance is not to be matched in the whole of Ireland. I married you for three reasons, as you well know. The first reason was that I had to have a mate who was as generous as I, and that you are. The second, I had to have a man who was as brave in battle as I, and that you are. Thirdly, I had to have a man who was without jealousy, for you know that one man will never satisfy me for long, nor a score. When I have one man between my thighs I am already thinking of the next, and whether his behind will be big or small and other things that give me delight.

"Now, all these things you have. You are neither mean nor timid nor jealous. It was certainly not for wealth that I married you. Why, I could match cow with cow, cooking pot with cooking pot, fork with fork and feather with feather when I came to you. You are not forgetting I had already been the wife for many years of Conchobor of Ulster and got much wealth from him before I ever thought or heard of you."

Ailill said nothing.

"Wake up!" his wife cried. "All night you vexed me with your remark, and now you think to snore through the day. Tell me one thing you have in the way of wealth whose exact twin or better I do not possess. An end to snoring now. This is an important matter."

There was nothing for the poor man to do but to wake up thoroughly. Medb began immediately to recount all her possessions, not forgetting to mention that she was the daughter of the High King of Ireland and had brought to her husband Ailill a very rich wedding present.

"Clothing for twelve men," she said, "and two pairs of shoes for each. A war chariot worth seven women slaves. Enough red gold to cover your face from ear to ear. Enough light-colored gold to weigh as much as your arm. Also my father gave me a whole province of Ireland, this selfsame province of Cruachan in Connaught and this selfsame fort in which you now live. You also had my talented body, supple and strong, and all the experience I brought to your bed for your delight. It is plain that my fortune is greater than yours, and you had no right to vex me all night with your remark."

"No one in all Ireland has more property, more weapons, more jewels, more precious hoards of cups and torques and breast cups and other treasure than I," he said. "That is a commonly accepted fact. You are out of your wits to challenge it."

"I do challenge it," she cried. "I do. I do." She was so angry she thumped him on his muscular shoulder and called for a steward, who came tumbling into the bedchamber. A man past his prime he was, his legs spindly and his belly large.

"Recount immediately everything I owned when I married the king," she said. "Start with the kitchenware."

"And match it with everything I own," said Ailill.

"The stranger shall judge which is finer or whether they are equal," said Medb, pointing to me. "Bring samples of each." She beckoned to me. "Come sit upon the bed and you may do as you please," she said. "Do not be ashamed of the presence of my husband. He is well used to sharing, and a generous man."

She moved over on the bed.

The steward started his accounting by listing the smallest and least worthy stuff—swill buckets, buckets for water, tubs for beer, flesh forks, knives, caldrons, drinking pots, salt boxes and so on. Samples were produced and taken away again. But for each one Medb had, Ailill had the match.

Then came clothes, and then ornaments such as finger rings and dyed cloths in every color—red, purple, blue, gold, green, gray, brown. Not a color was missing; and for each Medb had, Ailill again had the match.

They started on living things then. Five hundred speckled hens for Medb. Five hundred speckled hens, as plump and as pretty and as good layers, for Ailill. Then heads of cattle and horses and sheep. But for every ewe and ram, milch cow and heifer—brown, white, black or spotted—owned by Medb, Ailill had the twin.

The cattle, however, were her undoing. After the cows came the counting of bulls—fathers of herds and source of all wealth. That same white bull which had conducted me to the chamber and was the biggest bull in all Connaught or Leinster or Munster belonged solely to Ailill. Medb had no match for it.

"You are beaten, and properly," said Ailill. "Beaten by a bull—a big tool and balls to match—something a woman, you in particular, can use and enjoy, but do not possess. No need for this Greek to give judgment. My bull has beaten you and as I said last night, it is well to be the wife of a wealthy man."

But Medb was not the woman to accept defeat. "Let Fergus Mac Roth be brought here this minute," she said to the steward. This was the man from whom Conchobor had taken the throne of Ulster, though I had last seen him at Conchobor's court. Yet here he was in rival Connaught.

Fergus was there in a moment, massive, black-bearded, brooding still.

"You who were King of Ulster and rightly should be so," said Medb, "must know the herds of that fair land across the Boann water. Tell me now, in all of Ulster is there not one bull to match the great white bull that by luck and not good grace belongs to my husband?"

"There is indeed," said Fergus. "He is the only match for that white bull. You will find him in the territory of Cuailnge, in the lands belonging to Daire Mac Fiachna's house. A brown bull, he is, and as big or bigger than Finnbennach, the white one. His horns cleave the sky. Happy the owner of such a beast."

"I must have him," cried Medb. "I must have him." She

beat like a spoiled brat on her husband's back, which he had turned toward her, for he desired to finish his sleep.

"Well, have him then," said Ailill. "Whatever is needed, we will do."

"Go immediately to Daire and ask him to lend me the Brown Bull of Cuailnge, the Donn Cuailnge, for a year."

"He is a courteous and generous man," said Fergus. "But he would not lend it to you for a day. Who indeed would loan such an unmatched beast to a queen with a mighty host on the other side of Ireland from him? Suppose, which is not something unreasonable to the imagination, suppose you fell in love with this bull? Suppose you decided that you could not be parted from it. What then could Daire do?"

"What nonsense you talk," said Medb. "Am I not a queen? Will I not give him my royal pledge that at the end of the year he shall have his bull back? Is not that enough?"

"With such a pledge and such arguments I lost a kingdom —a fact well known to Daire and to all Ulster," said Fergus.

"Then I will give presents also—hire the bull for a year. I will give him fifty heifers, each a year old, the delights of any bull in Ireland, and when their udders fill, they will satisfy a thousand every day with their milk. My own strain of cattle I am talking of. He will get the bull back with the heifers. And if Daire himself will come with the bull, to see to its safekeeping, I will give him an area of the Plain of Ai, the richest part of the plain, equal to all the lands he possesses. I will give him a chariot worth twenty-one slave girls—yes, three times the wedding gift I gave to my snoring husband here. And on top of that I will give him my own thighs for his pleasure as many times as he wishes and in whatever manner he wishes. You will have to agree that nothing could be more generous than that."

"Of the latter part of the bargain I can speak to him with warmth," said Fergus.

"You are not perfect as a lover, but you are certainly improving," said Medb. "But be on your way. Go immediately to Daire and put my bargain to him. An Ulsterman yourself, and properly king, you are certainly the best messenger I can send."

"I would like a thousand spears. . . ." said Fergus.

"You will take that one man there—the Greek, Uliseacht. None other. He is a magical man, I have heard. Wonderful things happen when he is present. Tell me, Uliseacht, what are you doing here in Ireland, land of the Sacred Celts, the people of Dana?"

"I seek my home in Ithaka," I replied. "The gods make sport of me and send me under enchantments to strange places, for I have offended great Poseidon, lord of the sea, and brother to mighty Zeus."

"Then you should be a great ally and friend to us," said Medb. "For it is often that we ourselves offend and challenge Poseidon, whom we call Manannan, son of Lir. Many times when he rages our warriors take arms and plunge, fighting mad, into his tremendous surf and battle him for hours and even days. We would wrest his secrets and his treasures from him. Have no fear that you have offended him. All Ireland battles Manannan. We defy his storms and his rages and delight to taunt him with the lightest craft, launched into the boiling seas he raises in his tempests."

To hear the great god defied so openly made me quake with fear. Certainly in this mad land into which I have been cast, I decided, there is no wisdom. Wisdom starts with fear of the gods. But I said nothing, though inwardly offering a prayer to Zeus that he would recognize the innocence of my heart in that I did not partake in this defiance of his brother Poseidon.

"Manannan, whom you call Poseidon, lives on an island between here and Alba which is for that reason called the

Island of Manannan," continued Medb. "One day we will assemble our warriors and attack him in his home and drag him out and with him that great serpent of the seas which is his pet."

I remained silent, cursing the thought that in my ten years since the fall of Troy I should now be among blasphemers whose want of reverence for the gods would certainly fall on me.

Medb, a bold, vixenish, blasphemous woman, though beautiful, now told Fergus to go and me to stay. "Tell me, Uliseacht," she said, gently combing my beard with her fingernails, for we were still side by side upon the bed. "Tell me, Uliseacht, is there a Greek way in love play? I love to learn new things. Old ways are soon stale. Surely you crafty Greeks have thought of something novel."

Nothing to do then but satisfy her. As an eel, hooked, writhes and twists itself upon the line, so she writhed and twisted about during the encounter. She had enough vigor to have taken half, perhaps all, of the men in her kingdom, of whatever age. I wondered whether she were not some sea nymph like Calypso, herself insatiable in the matter of men. Her name meant mare.

CHAPTER

10

WE SET OUT THAT SAME DAY, ON MEDB'S
order, for in everything she was impetuous.
We took the travel chariot of Fergus Mac
Roth, its carriage of basketwork, its floor of
yew. Of alder wood were the wheels, of heart
of oak the axle bearing. Two stallions pulled the chariot, surg-
ing forward mile upon mile as storm winds sweep over the sea.
A sea of stones we first traversed, but not slowly like Tyrian
merchants picking their careful way with loaded carts to a
fair. No, we surged and banged and bumped and clattered
over these stones, scarce able to keep our feet in the plunging

chariot, which at times rode on one stout wheel alone, and then upon the other.

Fergus goaded the stallions to their greatest speed. He hoped to pitch me off my feet and perhaps out of the chariot, to break my head upon the stones. He had little hope of success. I have seen the foaming breakers burst yard high over my black ship, I have seen the quartering seas rock and batter her lovely hull, the prow now buried and then the stern, the oarsmen gone for a moment in the wall of spray. I have had her keeled over by sudden blasts so that she floated on her side, stricken by the wrath of some god, the rowers tumbled off the benches and into the churning ocean. All these things I have seen and kept my feet upon her deck. No chariot, then, would knock me to my knees or over the side.

When Fergus had done his best with the goad, I took it from him, shouting that his steeds had no real blood and he no skill at chariot urging. Harder I drove those foam-flecked stallions, until their flanks streamed blood. Fergus gripped the sides of the chariot, his knuckles white, and cried, "Let us stop and eat."

So when we had stopped and unspanned the stallions and set them to grass, he said, "There are more stones in Connaught than in any land in the world."

"No one who is far traveled would say that," I replied. "In Ithaka, what you call stones here, we call pebbles. Our chariots —bigger, heavier than these frail flower baskets of yours—we dash over mountains. Yes, from hot sunny ground to frost-rimmed peaks we gallop them."

"You are too bold with your tongue and your boasts," cried Fergus.

"He who has lost his kingdom to a boy should not reprimand one who helped to level Troy," I replied. "It is no eager youth armed yesterday who travels with you, but a warrior of twenty years. None other than he who was judged most worthy to receive the battle gear of Achilles when that great hero fell."

"Achilles I do not know and cannot speak of," said Fergus. "I have yet to see you play your part in any bloody fray."

A herd of red deer grazed nearby. "I will put on a stalking skin and cut the throat of a pretty doe for our dinner," said Fergus.

"Save yourself such trouble," I replied and, taking my bow case, removed the mighty stave, strung it, nocked an arrow to the string and brought the doe down so suddenly the rest of the herd stood like statues to see her fall, uncertain of what had happened.

So we feasted on venison and talked first of Medb, who had sent us on our errand.

"She has a will strong as death," said Fergus. "It sickens me to see how she runs her king, Ailill himself, backward and forward round and about, like a good-natured boy. He is too lazy to rule and leaves all to her. He has two brothers who are kings. 'They do not rule wisely,' he says. 'Why should I pretend that I could do better?' So he leaves all things to Medb, who often fills his place in the bed with other men. She has a behind that an army would follow, panting."

"That is a dangerous state of affairs," I said. "Agamemnon, our leader in the Trojan wars, returning home victorious and full of plunder, with every honor a warrior could achieve, was struck down, his throat cut, in his own house by his plotting wife. I saw his soul in the Place of the Dead which I visited on my wanderings, not yet concluded. Hear what he said:

"I warn you. Never give way to a woman
Nor trust one, however dear, nor tell
Her all. Some little things a man may
Tell his dearest wife. Others, graver,
He should cover up. Nor plainly return to
Her after long voyaging. Secretly appear.

Slowly, with stealth, reveal your presence—
Or keep it hid.
Beds too long solitary are often filled.
When the Wandering Man returns he may
Find lies and murder for his welcome,
His own hot blood the wine served
For his home-coming."

"Are not your Greek women as free as your men?" asked Fergus, his mouth full of bloodied venison, for we were too hungry to blacken the flesh well with fire.

"After marriage it is proper in the Greek lands for the woman to remain faithful to her husband."

"Who would want for a wife a woman that no other man lies with?" asked Fergus. "It's something beyond thought. Here we ring the changes loud and often, man and wife, and have our full joy of life. Were I and a few others in Ithaka, we would cheer some lonely wives, I tell you."

"I tell you only what is thought proper for outward appearances," I said. "Not what is done. Yet trouble comes of that kind of thing. It was because of Helen, hot as a spring ewe, that thousands died at Troy. Off she went with Paris, full of lust for that handsome fellow, her husband Menelaus being away—and brought death and doom to every noble house in Greece."

"In all the four kingdoms of Ireland, nothing so foolish would ever happen," said Fergus. "A bull we might fight about," he added slyly. "A woman, never. There are always others though I must say that, although all are made the same, each has some special charm. So the gods willed it to keep men lusty and women fertile."

"I know why you are in Connaught instead of Ulster," I said. "Your throne was taken by Conchobor with the aid of his father, the druid Cathbad. But I saw others of Ulster about the palace of Medb. At least they wore the three-horned helmet and squared shield of Conchobor's men. What are they doing? Is some mischief planned?"

"You do not know how I came to be in Connaught at all," replied Fergus. "It is true that I was tricked out of my throne by Cathbad so that his son, Conchobor, by Nessa the White Mare, who became my mate for a while, could reign. But if you will remember that bargain, the boy was to hold power only for a year and at the end of that time, I was to be received again as King of Ulster."

"True," I said. "Yet Conchobor is now king for all time."

"Through the stratagems of Cathbad and Nessa," said Fergus, scowling. "What man is equal to the plots of a wizard and a woman?" He picked up a bone of the deer and smashed it with the pommel of his great sword and then sucked out the yellow marrow, blobs of which fell on his thick black beard.

"It was just like that that Cathbad, Nessa and the boy Conchobor smashed me and sucked me dry," he said. "The bargain was that he was to hold power for a year. In that year whatever he asked was to be done. He was not king for a month before he turned to me and said, 'Give me all the glittering arms in your arms house, for they are mine now.' Nothing to do but grant that request, for it is the law that in all things the king must be obeyed.

"Next Conchobor, after consulting with Nessa, said, 'Give me the key to your treasure house. The rich armbands of red gold, the breast cups of gold and silver, the drinking cups of creamy skulls with jewels set in them, the necklaces of gold spheres for the horses' trappings—all these things are for me, for I am king.'

" 'I was a fool to agree to such a bargain as this,' I said. 'For one hundredth part of what I have already given to you, I could have every woman in Ireland in my bed.'

" 'Look to the future,' said crafty Nessa. 'When you are

king again, you may have everything back.' With that I had to be comforted.

"Then Conchobor required of the women of the court that they give him half of their jewelry. To show that there was no malice or favoritism Nessa added to this all that she had received from every warrior who had sought her. When the boy Conchobor had received all the arms and all the treasure and the greater part of the jewelry of the women, he called together all the warriors of Ulster.

" 'These things are for you,' he said. It was Cathbad who advised him. 'Here for Furbaide is a winged helmet set with rare blue stones and crowned with a raven in red gold. Here for Cuscraid is the blue-bladed sword Slaughterer. Many a heap of steaming bowels has it made. Cormac, yours is the long-shafted spear, Croda the Cruel One. Noisiu of the Strong Arm, certainly you may rejoice. For you I have saved what is fitting—a two-handed battle ax of bronze. Many a man it has cleaved from skull to crotch with one blow in the hands of Fergus himself.'

"Every month he did not fail to call the warriors together, hold a great feast and give them such treasures.

"The great drinking vats he kept full of wine and of honey beer. The cooking caldrons likewise were kept bubbling with the flesh of the boar, and the flesh forks always close by so that a tasty morsel could be taken out without trouble.

"At the end of the year, however, it was I who assembled the warriors. 'My pledge is fulfilled,' I said. 'I am your king again.'

" 'This is not to be decided in a moment,' said Celtchar, the Opener of Battles. 'We have a weighty problem to deal with here.'

" 'My kingdom was pledged for a year only, so that Nessa, my chief wife, might say her son was king and so his son might be called son of a king. That is all the weight there is in it,' I replied.

" 'The pledge is a feather. The weight is more than a thousand men can lift,' said Conall Cernach.

" 'Explain,' I said, seating myself on a stool and putting my sword across my knees.

" 'Easily done,' said Conall Cernach, doing the same. We sat knee to knee, swords drawn, facing each other.

" 'You sold your kingdom for a woman—that is the feather's weight, for surely a kingdom is worth more than a woman,' said Conall.

" 'It was to fulfill the tradition that the king must mate with a white mare,' I said. 'Also, you were one of those who urged the bargain on me.'

" 'That is no lie,' said Conall Cernach. 'All agree you speak truly there. You sold your kingdom for a year for a woman. But now your kingdom has been bought by Conchobor for all time. That is the weighty matter. One thousand men will not lift that weight. Look at them. See which one will help you.'

"I looked around. No man would help me. All had been bought by the gifts of Conchobor.

" 'There are a hundred thousand men in Connaught who can change the business,' I said.

" 'Let them come so that we may bathe in each other's hot blood,' said Celtchar, the Opener of Battles.

" 'They will come,' I said, and left. I called for my chariot and charioteer, armed, and set out for Connaught. On the way I met that white mare Nessa.

" 'A parting kiss,' I cried to her, and struck off her head with my sword. The blood spurted from her neck.

" 'You did well, Fergus Mac Roth,' said my charioteer. 'I will tie her by the legs and drag the body down the road and throw it into the river.' So he did, and then I remembered the rest of the scheming Cathbad's story, and got into the pool in the river where she lay, and drank the water stained with her blood and so fulfilled the last part of the tradition the wizard had told me of—namely, that the king, having mated with the mare, must drink of the soup made of her flesh and blood."

This barbarous tale I received in silence. Then I said, "What of the rest of the men of Ulster now at the court of Connaught? Were these loyal men who followed you, their deposed king?"

"They are here because of Derdriu of the Sorrows," said Fergus.

"The name, alas, means nothing to me, a stranger," I said. "However, if you will tell me something of her story to pass away the time I will, in return, at some convenient hour, likewise tell you a tale of my own wanderings or the adventures of others that may amuse you."

Fergus stared dully at the fire, the fat from the venison gleaming in the yellow light of the flames on his black beard.

"She was the curse of Ulster and indeed of Ireland, though the most beautiful woman that ever lived in this land."

"Then she must have been like Helen who brought down Troy and with its fall loss and sorrow to all the Greeks," I said.

Fergus kicked at a sod which had fallen out of the fire, sending a sheet of sparks whirling up into the air. "Better she had never been born," he said.

CHAPTER

11

ERGUS NOW CALLED BACK HIS TWO STALLIONS WITH A loud whistle. He staked them out, one on the north and one on the south of the camp.

"None are so impious as to attack in the dark along the road of the sun," he said. "That is from the east or the west. Even in Connaught. So the stallions will guard north and south while we talk, for I will tell you the tale of Derdriu. When we sleep, you may take which side you choose to guard, your weapons beside you."

"Surely none would be so lacking in courage as to attack sleeping warriors?" I said.

"None of our kind," said Fergus grimly. "There are others. The Men of the Bogs, or the Belly Men or the Men of the Earth. They are all the same men. They cut throats by night."

"And who are they? No spirit can hurt a man. That I well know, for I have with my sword held them off a trench full of blood for which they slavered in their dark abode."

"They are the people who were here before we, the Sons of Dana, came," said Fergus. "They live in caves and under the ground and in the middle of the bogs, where charioteers and warriors may not get them. Like hungry dogs, they raid by night. They are most numerous in this part."

These precautions having been taken, Fergus started his tale.

"It was in the spring of the year," he said. "Conchobor and his warriors were drinking in the house of his storyteller, none other than Fedlimid, Son of Fate. His wife was helping to serve the men, who were in but the second stage of drunkenness. The wife of Fedlimid, though pregnant, had carried many gallons of wine and beer about for her guests. She was sent by her husband to help bring in another great jar of wine with which the women were struggling.

"As she was crossing the great hall on this errand a scream, terrifying to hear, came from her womb. Some said it was like the scream of hunting eagles diving to rip the eyes from a lamb. Some said it was like the scream of a man flung off the Great Cliffs for cowardice under arms—the scream he gives as he sees below him the lacy foam and the rocks on which his body will be smashed. Some say it was the scream given by some of the skulls in Conchobor's Gory House when a particular peril is expected. Certain it is that that scream struck black, quaking fright into the hearts of all in that hall, myself among them.

"The oldest warrior present was Sencha Mac Ailella. It was his duty, then, to first recover his courage. 'Seize that woman,' he cried. 'Bring her before her husband. Make her stand upright in front of him and boldly and truthfully tell us what was the cause and meaning of that scream. If not we should cut her throat this moment.'

"So the woman was seized and brought before Fedlimid.

'Woman,' he said.
You have put a great fright

((94))

On the guests of our house.
A grave discourtesy.
What caused that horrible cry
To come from your womb?
Speak truly.
You stand before warriors,
And Ulster's king.'

She replied.

'Husband of my delight,
Son of the Fates,
Prince among storytellers,
If your mind
Can not catch the meaning
Of that terrible sound
How am I to know?
Who am but
The dull mirror
Of yourself?
What woman knows for sure
What she carries
In her womb?
Man, or woman
Or other Being?
Let Cathbad
Prince of Seers
Piercer of Darkness
Who knows all roads,
Let Cathbad
Say who screamed.
He alone should know.'

"Cathbad fixed his close-set eyes upon the woman and, leaving his place, moved to her. He lifted up her gown and put his hand upon her womb to feel whatever lay behind that strong wall of flesh.

((95))

" 'What do you say?' demanded Conchobor, his face still pale, for to him the scream had sounded like the terrified neighing of a horse finding a serpent coiled in the straw of its stall.

"Cathbad said:

> *'Hair like sunlight*
> *Caught in honey*
> *Eyes of mystery*
> *Like mountain lakes,*
> *Flesh white*
> *As drifts of snow,*
> *Cheeks aglow*
> *As swathes of foxgloves.*
> *A woman child*
> *Lies in the womb.*
> *Chariot warriors*
> *Lie in heaps for her.*
> *High kings*
> *Lust for her.*
> *High queens*
> *Tremble because*
> *They have not*
> *Her beauty.*
> *Strife and division*
> *Her fate.*
> *Her name*
> *Derdriu of the Sorrows.'*

" 'The woman should be killed,' cried Sencha, the old warrior. 'Foolish the fighter who awaits the blow. Lop off her head and save the kingdom.'

"He drew his sword to behead the woman.

" 'Hold,' cried Conchobor. 'She is not to be touched.' He said this because the terrible cry to him had sounded like the neighing of a horse. He was himself, as you know, the son of the mare-woman, Nessa.

" 'Speak carefully,' said Sencha. 'Your one word may cause the death of five thousand chariot warriors, as Cathbad has foretold.'

" 'Let her live,' said Conchobor.

"Hardly a moment later the child was born.

"Cathbad reached for the child and the mother gave it to him: a golden-haired girl, bloodied and bruised by the battle for birth.

"He held her up for all to see.

" 'Sorrow follows this child,' he said. 'Fergus exiled. The three sons of Uisliu exiled too. Ulster torn. Graves on every hand. Kings in contention. That is her story.'

" 'Kill her,' the warriors cried. 'Let Sencha save us all with one swift blow.'

" 'No,' cried Conchobor. 'A danger foreseen is a danger averted. There is more than one way. I myself will rear this child. I myself will keep watch over her. She shall see none but me and her serving women. I myself shall marry her. It is the part of the king to ward off the sorrow of the nation.'

"Cathbad looked at him from his narrow-set eyes. 'Conchobor the Fool,' he said. 'Ever the fool.' "

Fergus fell silent. He contented himself with staring gloomily at the fire. The two tethered stallions tore at the grass in the silence, and I could hear the swish of their tails as they drove the horseflies from their goaded withers. The one to the south of us neighed and the hand of Fergus slipped swiftly to his sword hilt, though he continued staring at the fire. For myself, I do not believe in sitting in the glow of a fire to make a target for an arrow from the dark. I lay back swiftly and, rolling over onto my belly, crawled toward the stallion to peer into the darkness and listen. But that foolish horse had returned to its cropping and had neighed for no reason.

After a while Fergus spoke again.

"I would delight to have the head of Cathbad hanging from my belt," he said. "He it was who cost me my kingdom, so that I became a mere warrior in the court of that boy Conchobor he fathered on the mare-woman."

"A moment," I said. "You say you were there at the birth of Derdriu. Yet I thought you had, after taking your revenge on Nessa, left Ulster for Connaught, seeking warriors to wrest back the lordship of Ulster."

"So I did," said Fergus. "And all I got for my travels was Ailill too lazy to go to war and Medb too lustful to get out of bed. I spent six days and six nights with her—three for my own satisfaction, the six for her. Her breasts are so big no man can take more than a third of one in his mouth at one time. Then I went back to Ulster, of which I am true king. Medb would not fight for a throne." He paused and said, "Such a woman would fight only for a bull."

He glanced slyly at me. "Is it true that in Greece where you come from, Uliseacht, women copulate with bulls?"

"Not the Greeks," I said. "No such bestiality would be permitted among the Greeks. But, according to legend at least, something of the sort seems to have gone on in ancient times on one of our islands."

"It would take a bull to satisfy Medb," Fergus said.

"Tell me more of Derdriu," I asked.

"Conchobor the Fool—that is what Cathbad said of him," said Fergus. "A fool he is, too, never growing to be a full man. He thought he could keep Derdriu of the Sorrows separated and apart from all men in Ulster. Seal a woman up from birth in the middle of a mountain, and there is still some man who will hew his way through the granite rocks and find her. Such treasure men will not be denied.

"Derdriu was reared in seclusion by Conchobor, seeing only women, and grew to be the most beautiful woman in Ireland. Her skin was as white as the flesh of an apple. Her hair was sunlight braided. Her voice was so melodious it silenced the birds. Even the piping blackbird of spring fell quiet as Derdriu spoke. Roses and other flowers stretched toward her as she walked through her garden. The grass embraced and reverently kissed her bare feet. The only man she was allowed to see other than Conchobor was Leborcham the satirist. He was a tall man, but hunchbacked. He threatened to satirize Conchobor all over Ulster, Ireland and Gaul if he was not allowed to see Derdriu. Thinking no danger from so misshapen a man, Conchobor let him be her companion.

"One day, in midwinter, it was necessary to kill a milk-fed calf whose mother's udders were dry; there was no forage to keep the mother through to the new grass. Leborcham took the calf out into the snow and quickly cut its throat. The blood spurted on the snowy ground and a raven had soon alighted and started pecking at the blood-drenched snow.

" 'Ah, that I could find one man of such coloring,' said Derdriu. 'One with hair as black as the raven, skin as white as the snow and cheeks as red as the blood.'

" 'Not far to look,' said Leborcham. 'None other than Noisiu, son of Uisliu, who lives nearby.'

" 'My heart aches to meet him,' said Derdriu.

" 'Beltaine is courting time,' said the satirist.

"So it happened that at Beltaine, when the grass was new and seeded with daisies and the trees and hedges full of singing birds, the three sons of Uisliu passed often by Emain Macha, where Derdriu was kept. She heard them singing and peered at them over the wall of her garden, and her eyes fell most often on Noisiu with his black hair, his skin as white as the flesh of an apple and his cheeks red as blood.

"One day Noisiu passed by alone, and Derdriu, with the help of the satirist, slipped out quickly from her garden. She lay in the grass at a place where Noisiu must find her, her hair spread around her like a golden cloak.

" 'A lovely flower I see before me,' said Noisiu when he saw her.

" 'Shame on you then if you will not pluck it for your own,' said Derdriu.

" 'That flower belongs to another,' said Noisiu.

" 'The flower belongs to him to whom it is offered,' said Derdriu. 'Would you stand before the warriors of Ulster and let it be known you shrank from the plucking?'

" 'That would be shame indeed,' said Noisiu.

" 'Bend then and pluck the flower,' said Derdriu, and pulled him gently down to her.

"Then his two brothers came and saw what was done.

" 'You have taken the king's rose,' they said.

" 'Would you rather I was without manhood and the rose unplucked?' asked Noisiu, and explained what had happened.

" 'We must flee,' said the brothers. 'Others will join us. But Ulster is no safe place.'

"They fled with three times fifty warriors and three times fifty women to attend them. Conchobor, hearing what had happened, sounded his war horn, beat upon his shield and chased them the length and breadth of Ireland. From the red waterfall of Es Ruaid in the southwest of Ireland to the Mountain of Etair in the northwest of Ireland he chased them, sometimes only two breadths of a horse from them. Yet he could not catch them.

"Then they fled to the King of Alba across the water and offered themselves and their warriors as fighting men for his service. But they kept Derdriu hidden from the King of Alba for her great beauty, and built her a house in such a way that no one could see her in or around it.

"The King of Alba gladly accepted their swords and spears and chariots. But he had a steward whose job it was to find out everything that the king might want to know. Secretly he peeked into the house of Noisiu and saw him lying there with golden-haired Derdriu in his arms.

" 'There is a woman with Noisiu, who is fit to be the wife of the king of the whole world,' said the steward. 'Why not set on the camp suddenly and take her? There are only three times fifty warriors between her and your bed. A small barrier for such a delight.'

" 'They are good fighting men all,' said the King of Alba. 'I would not have one of them killed except in my own battles and on my side. Go instead to the woman every day and secretly suggest that she lie with me. That is the best way to arrange such a matter.'

" 'She is faithful only to Noisiu,' said the steward.

" 'No woman is faithful who is constantly beseeched,' said the king. 'Go.'

"Every day the steward came to Derdriu with his proposal, but Derdriu told Noisiu about it each night. When that failed the sons of Uisliu and all their warriors were constantly sent into the most dangerous parts of battles, and traps were set for them to kill them off so the king could lie with Derdriu. But they loved battle and slaughter and the three sons of Uisliu grew strong on it and pleaded for more. So that plan failed.

"In the end the King of Alba decided nothing could be done unless the sons of Uisliu and their accompanying warriors were all killed off. All his men were to gather and not stop the attack until there was no one left alive except Derdriu.

" 'We must flee tonight,' Derdriu told Noisiu when she heard of this. 'If we do not, nothing will be left of you or your brothers or those with us. I will be bound and carried to the king's bed.'

" 'Because of that threat alone we consent to flee,' said Noisiu. 'But if it were a mere matter of slaughter, we would stay here and bloody the hills of Alba with the warriors of the King of Alba.' They fled then to an island between Alba and Ireland. There they settled for a while. News of them was brought to Conchobor.

" 'A shameful thing if such fine men should fall into the

hands of their enemies with their own king and all his host of warriors close to hand,' said Dubthach, the Dark One. 'Do you desert your fighting men because Derdriu chose another bed?'

" 'Better to forgive the sons of Uisliu and have them by your side at the next assault—wherever it may be—than fill their places with men less stout at the shield wall,' said Sencha, the Old One.

" 'A woman costs you three such swords—not to speak of the others who accompanied them,' said Conall Cernach. 'What woman is worth that price?'

" 'Send for them,' said Conchobor. 'They will be given guarantees of safety.'

"Messengers then went to the three on the sea-girt island where they had built a fortress.

" 'We will come back,' said Noisiu, 'if the king sends guarantees of safety.'

" 'What guarantees?' said the messengers.

" 'Let Fergus Mac Roth come and let Dubthach, the Dark One, come and let Conchobor's son Cormac come. If they will come pledged to defend us and keep us and Derdriu safe, we will joyfully return to Ulster of the pleasant green hills.'

" 'Do not say so,' said Derdriu. 'Better to die here on this well-fortified island than trust the word of that king.'

" 'It is not to his word that we trust, but to that of the mightiest and most honorable warriors in the land—Fergus Mac Roth, Dubthach and Cormac, the king's own son. Not to go, given these pledges, would be to deny honor itself.'

" 'We go to our deaths,' said Derdriu. But they would not hear her.

"So the three sons of Uisliu, with Derdriu and their war companions, returned to Ulster and made straight to Emain Macha. But Conchobor the cunning, who took my own land from me by a stratagem, had laid a plot for them.

"I had laid on me, the day I took arms, certain pledges

which I could not ignore, whatever the price. The first and most sacred of these was that invited to an ale feast, I must never refuse, whatever the reason. The same pledge was laid on Dubthach, that he must not dishonor himself as a warrior by refusing hospitality. We were hardly a day on our road to Emain Macha when he and I were invited to six ale feasts.

"We were bound by a warrior's honor to attend these feasts. The sons of Uisliu would not wait out the needed time for the ale feasts. They had made a vow to go to Emain Macha without stopping on the road to look to right or to left until they saw, rising on the hills before them, the three palaces of Conchobor.

"On they went, then. I sent my own son Fiacha with them in my place. It was no niggardly exchange. Left-handed he had cleaved many a skull from crown to chin with one stroke.

"At last the sons of Uisliu saw rising on the green hills before them the three palaces of Conchobor.

" 'Home at last and no harm,' said Noisiu. 'Foolish the fears of women.'

" 'My heart is dead already,' replied Derdriu. 'We breathe our last of this world's air.'

" 'Conchobor has given a king's pledge of safety,' said Noisiu.

" 'So the hawk pledges the dove and then eats out its brains,' said Derdriu. 'Turn back while there is yet time.'

" 'That would be dishonorable,' said Noisiu.

"On they went until they came to the green plain in the middle of which, on a hilltop, Emain Macha stood.

"Conchobor had with him at the time Eogan Mac Durthacht, King of Fernmag. He had come to make his peace with Conchobor.

" 'Peace you may have,' said Conchobor. 'But first kill me the sons of Uisliu and bring me Derdriu whom I raised for my own bed.'

" 'Gladly,' said Eogan. 'But have you no warriors of your own?'

" 'Many, as you well know,' replied Conchobor. 'But I have pledged that I will do no harm to the sons of Uisliu. A king may not break his word.'

" 'Agreed,' said Eogan. 'I will do as you wish as a pledge of peace between us.' He went out across the plain with his warriors to meet Noisiu and Derdriu. My own son Fiacha, suspecting treachery, moved to Noisiu's side—a shield for his sword arm. The women watched from the walls.

" 'A thousand welcomes home,' cried Eogan. 'May you never leave again.' Then with a swift thrust of his great spear, he broke the back of Noisiu, who toppled to the ground. Fiacha, my own son, threw himself across him, his own body as a shield as he had pledged.

"Noisiu was killed with spearthrusts through the body of my son. A glorious end. Happy the man who fathers such a warrior.

"Then the battle broke out all over the plain. Down went the other two brothers, down went the three times fifty men who had accompanied them into exile. Nothing remained of that gallant host but slashed and headless bodies. Many an arm was found with the sword tight clenched in the bloody hand. Derdriu was seized, bound, and brought before Conchobor.

" 'Another weapon I have reserved for you,' he said. 'A sword thirsty for entry.'

"Derdriu wept for shame, and grief.

"Word came to me and to Dubthach of this treachery. So Ulster was divided because of that woman. Many the battles we fought—Ulsterman against Ulsterman; the men of Fergus against the men of Conchobor.

"Emain Macha I set on fire with my own hands. Dubthach massacred all the girls of Ulster that Conchobor might be hungry for his favorite food.

"Warriors fell like sparrows in a hailstorm. The mountains trembled before our wrath. Rivers receded at our approach. Still we could not best the men of Conchobor. At last with one thousand of the men of Ulster I left for Connaught to live in exile with Ailill and Medb. Those are the warriors you saw and asked me about and it was because of Derdriu of the Sorrows and not because of the scheming of Cathbad that I myself am now in Connaught instead of in my Kingdom of Ulster.

"Now, at the bidding of Medb, I return to Ulster to seek what she most desires and what most suits her—a bull."

"What of Derdriu?" I asked.

"Better she had been killed at birth as Sencha advised," said Fergus bitterly. "A cold grave under the stones her gift to many a man. Conchobor kept her a year. Little joy she gave him, for he had to force his way between her thighs. At last he said to her, 'Whom do you hate more—myself or Eogan Mac Durthacht?'

" 'Eogan Mac Durthacht, who killed Noisiu, the breath of my life.'

" 'Then go live a year with Eogan Mac Durthacht,' said Conchobor.

"She was bound and put in Eogan's chariot. Great his delight to receive so lovely a playmate. Eogan goaded the stallions of his chariot to quickly travel the miles between him and his bedchamber. They crossed the Plain of Macha. There a great stone had been raised to Noisiu. The chariot passed close by.

" 'I come to you, delight of my eyes,' cried Derdriu. She leaned out of the chariot and her brains were splattered against the stone. That was the end of her. Her gift to Ireland was Ulster divided, the Sons of Uisliu dead, my own son dead, and the land seeded with the graves of warriors.

"Derdriu of the Sorrows—well named by Cathbad before her birth."

CHAPTER

12

CHOSE TO SLEEP ON THE SOUTH SIDE, WHERE THE HOBBLED stallion lay stretched in the starlight. Sword in hand, shield across the chest—so the warrior sleeps in the open. Venus trembled bright above the loom of a distant hill. To her I prayed.

"Goddess of love, immortal, generous Venus
Comforter of all wandering men,
Hear now the prayer of Ulysses,
Separated by the fish-filled oceans
And the wrath of the lord Poseidon
From his home and hearth in Ithaka.

> *Grant, full-breasted goddess,*
> *Generous mistress of gods and men,*
> *A safe return from this dark land*
> *To my own bright home among the Achaean crags.*
> *Let the love I bear my wife*
> *Be my offering to you."*

This prayer said, and the fire a dying jewel on the dark earth, I fell asleep.

A stench so strong I thought the stallion had pissed nearby awoke me. A little wind stirred out of the south. It brought with it the smell of urine. The stallion, standing, ears pricked forward, awaited whatever approached.

The fool lies cowering in danger's path; the tried warrior slips aside. So I moved to a little gully I had noted in the dying light before we ate. Such watchfulness gives life to the wandering soldier. Concealed then, a shadow lying within a shadow, I parted the stiff grass on the gully's rim and watched the Stinking Ones approach. Belly Men, they were, or Earth Men or Bog Men, as Fergus had described them.

Stooped and crouched they came, their reek with them, silent as the tide. The stallion neighed and, teeth bared, eyes bright as sword pommels, lashed out with his fore hooves. Well aimed was that kick, for with it came a clumping sound and blood thick and hot splattered my face. Two shapes fell to the ground to be spurred by the stallion's hooves and then came more of the Earth Men crawling, stooping, carrying clubs and knives curved like the quarter moon.

Out then I charged with the cry of war, and out too came Fergus. Swift and fearless, he cut the stallion's hobble with a cunning touch of his great spear. The other, already freed by Fergus, had fled, and off went its mate to leave us two, back to back, to fight against this horde.

Now came great slaughter, the hot drops of blood falling

about like that rain which, sullen and heavy, accompanies the thunderstorm. Club against shield edge, sword against sword we fought, Fergus exulting with each thrust of his spear, for so these barbarians fight. But I, like all the Achaeans, fought with cunning, enjoying the snick of the sword through bone, the blossoming of death's drink on cleaved face and opened chest and belly. They were no cowards, that I must say in truth, though it is no great deed to attack in the dark two sleeping warriors. But when the attack was launched, they pressed it well, though fighting without true skill, and making a hissing sound like a nest of disturbed serpents.

Soon a pile of wounded and dead lay about us, and the ground was slippery with gore. The dead stank worse than the living. It seemed we fought rotting corpses, the fly-blown bodies of unburied men. Their flesh had no firmness. One seized my throat; the touch was cold as fish guts. I screamed and Fergus, quick to aid, dashed his shield into that Earth Man's jaw.

Soon I was bleeding from many wounds, and Fergus also. Slower our thrusts and parries now while they, ever reinforced, fought on with vigor.

Ghostly dawn alone saved us. To the east, in gravecloth gray, the sky lightened. One by one the Earth Men slipped away, until with a last whimper, their leader left, hissing and attempting one further blow. Then, wonderful indeed to relate, when we looked around, not one body lay before us on the ground where there had been a score. With the light they were gone, living and dead, leaving only, in the freshening air, the foul taint of their presence.

"What marvel is this?" I asked. "Were there not a hundred of them around us, pressing from all sides, and twenty at our feet? I felt them squelch beneath my boots."

"From the Earth they come. To the Earth they return," said Fergus. "Into the Earth they would drag us had I not come to your defense. Certainly, Uliseacht, you may talk loudly in the halls of warriors. I will support your boasting. But you must admit that without my great spear, you would not be now breathing the pleasant morning air."

"Nor you without my cunning and my sword, Fergus, son of the Wind Bag," I replied. "For the first blow struck was mine, and the last also. Your naked back I covered and the pile of their dead before me was twice that which fell to your great spear."

"Such talk is disgraceful from one who owes his life to me," said Fergus. "No true warrior would be guilty of this vain boasting. Or if he persisted he would, without the slightest doubt, be put immediately to the test."

"Let us put it to a test then," I said. "Is it your belief and do you openly assert that the wounds which you have received, you sustained solely in my defense, while those from which my own blood is streaming were not sustained in defending you?"

"In my anger I have said a dishonorable and childish thing," said Fergus. "Come, let us bathe our wounds in the river and press on to Ulster."

CHAPTER

13

THE HOUSE OF DAIRE, SON OF FIACHNA, WAS OF ONE hundred rooms all under one roof. Added to them was the Great Hall for banqueting and his own bedchamber, wherein he had a bed of gold wrought by the Smith Chulainn. A fine house—that cannot be denied. His farmlands extended over three vast plains and two mountain ranges. He had twice twenty herds of black cattle, twice twenty herds of white cattle and twice twenty herds of gray cattle. His sheep moved like summer clouds over the mountain slopes. It tore my heart to hear the bleating of those sheep and the lowing of the cattle. Such are the sounds of Ithaka whose grain-giving soil I had not seen for twenty years.

Two defensive walls of stone surrounded this great house; through the massive gate we urged the chariot. There was no delay in admitting Fergus Mac Roth, once King of Ulster, to this magnificent place. Nor was I, Uliseacht, unknown, having split the head of Conall Cernach and carved the Champion's Portion at the feast given by Chulainn for Conchobor and his warriors.

Daire, son of Fiachna, was no warrior. Among the Celts, in their rain-drenched land, the cattle raisers do no fighting, but leave that to the warriors. Here they differ from the Achaeans, for Laertes, my own father, carved out his own farm in Ithaka of the little valleys among the stones. A rich place he made of it too, with three or four times, without boasting, the whole farmland of Daire. Yet he was a valiant fighting man too, and of my own deeds under arms there is no reason for me to be humble. They are unexcelled. But Daire, like the fellow whose wife Macha had been sent to outrun the stallions of Conchobor, was a stranger to spear and sword unless his own lands were beset.

Of his hospitality I could not complain. A boar's throat was cut the moment of our arrival and chunks of it were soon roasting on a spit to stay our hunger. Wine there was in plenty, served in deep chalices made of human skulls, set around with silver, gold and jewels. Wine thus served, it is believed, brings with it the strength of the man whose skull forms the chalice.

Before feasting, however, we bathed in vast copper caldrons —Fergus in one and I in the other. Naked maidens, their tiny breasts sweetly budding, served us.

"Two years to the plowing," cried Fergus, holding one delicate nipple between thumb and finger. "Would I were the plowshare that opens that virgin earth."

"A year might suffice," said the young girl. "Indeed it is a pity to keep so fine a plow unused. Lack of work may dull its edge."

"In with you," said Fergus, "while we talk of that," and, picking her up, he put her in the caldron with him, while the others giggled and stood hopefully about. But I had not the lust of Fergus for these young things, and so disappointed them.

When we had bathed and clothed we dined on the roast boar, and Fergus drank copiously of the wine.

Now that we were bathed and clad in soft linen dyed the green of Chaldis, it was time to come to the point of our embassy. About this Daire now inquired. He was a broad, honest-looking fellow with red-gold hair which tumbled over his shoulders to mingle with his beard of like color. He looked like the oak in autumn, for which tree he was named.

Fergus had soon told him all, starting with the quarrel between Ailill and Medb.

"For the loan then of the Brown Bull of Cuailnge, famed throughout Ireland, for a year, Medb will pay fifty yearling heifers of her own stock. You shall have the bull back. Also if you yourself will come with the bull to Connaught, you shall have a portion of the Plain of Ai the spread of your own fine farmlands and forests here. You shall also have a chariot worth thrice seven bondmaidens. You shall have Medb in your bed as often as you wish to seal the bargain."

"That last completes the price," cried Daire joyfully. "I have often dreamed of the embrace of her splendid thighs. No woman in all Ireland, they say, is better. Tell Medb she shall have two bulls which is indeed what she seeks—the Donn Cuailnge and myself." He was so delighted that he jumped up and down on his cushioned seat. His vigor was such that the cushions broke at the seams and feathers fell about him like the snow.

"Tomorrow we start," he said. "I cannot wait long for my price."

Off he went then to spread the news of his good fortune, leaving Fergus and me to be entertained by his steward and servants—the former a graying, thin man with a quiet look.

"Yours is a good master," said Fergus to the steward. "I think it would be hard to find a better in the whole of Ulster."

"You would not have far to look," said the steward sourly. "It is well known that Conchobor, the king, is better."

"Granted," said Fergus. "But it was generous of your master to agree so quickly to give us the Donn Cuailnge. Certainly I had not hoped for so quick a successful end to my mission. On the other hand," he added slyly, "perhaps it is better to give quickly what might be taken in any case."

"The four parts of Ireland could not wrest that bull from my master Daire if he decided against the loan," said the steward.

"May blood spout from your mouth for such idle boasting," cried Fergus. "Connaught alone could wrest the bull from your master if he withheld his consent."

"Then I will tell him so," said the steward, and left.

"What foolish thing is this you are doing now?" I cried. "Truly the wine you drank has gone to your head. You have the embassy successfully completed with a few well-chosen words and promises. Then you insult the generosity of your host by saying he had no choice in the matter of lending the bull."

Fergus turned his great bearded and scarred face toward me. His eyes were dull with drinking. Yet the cunning showed through his thick words. "I spoke only the truth," he said. "What I said is well known to Daire and the whole of Ulster."

"Known it might be," I answered. "Said is another matter. You must leave every man room for his pride. You should take back those words."

"A lie may have to be swallowed," said Fergus. "Never the truth. In any case, I have a little plowing to do this night. Let Daire dream of that old pasture Medb. There is unturned new grass aplenty here for me to furrow."

Off he staggered with three giggling girls, shameless as

Naiads. But I, fearing the outcome of this mission, sought out Daire. There he was, sitting in his nightshirt on that golden bed, his face red with rage.

"Wine spoke in the voice of Fergus," I said. "It is a common thing in every land. Pay no attention to what he said, but generously loan the bull as you promised, and you will find Medb a fit companion for many a day and night. She will not disappoint you. That I can promise."

"The insult dissolves the bargain," said Daire. "No man says that I gave my famous treasure because I had to."

"It is not Medb nor yet Ailill who said that," I replied. "So great and generous a man as yourself will not be so unjust as to blame them. They are not responsible for the words of Fergus Mac Roth. Fairly Medb made you promises in return for the loan of the bull. Generously you accepted those promises. What then have the words of Fergus, spoken in wine, to do with a bargain between noble personages?"

"This and this alone," cried Daire, his rage not abated at all. "If he had not mentioned taking the bull by force, the thought would never have occurred to me nor to the whole of Ulster. But he did mention it. And now the whole of Ulster will think me shamed to give the bull in a bargain behind which lies a threat."

"But Medb herself had no such threat in mind and would not agree with the wild words of Fergus Mac Roth," I said.

"Whether she had such a thought in mind or not does not matter," cried Daire. "Tomorrow that thought will blow through the whole land like the wind. In the meanest hut of the poorest cow herder in Ulster it will be said that I gave the bull under threat, and I will not have such a thing said of myself, or my country, or of my king, Conchobor the Open-Handed. So let them try to take the bull if they can. They shall not have him otherwise."

"Are ten thousand men to die for twenty words?" I asked.

((114))

"Ten thousand and twenty times ten thousand if need be," cried Daire.

Nothing more was to be said. On the following day Fergus spoke to Daire again.

"What is said over wine and meat is not to be given weight," he said.

"What is said is said," replied Daire. "Take the bull if you can, by force or by cunning. You shall not have him otherwise."

Fergus looked about him at the splendid hall. "I will return with the warriors of Connaught and a thousand from Ulster at my back," he said. "Famous deeds will be done. A bull taken. A kingdom restored." Then he left.

"You failed in your mission," I said as we set out for Connaught.

"I failed in Medb's mission," said Fergus. "In my own, I succeeded."

CHAPTER

14

W E HAD SOON REACHED CONNAUGHT AND THE fortress palace of Ailill and Medb at Cruachan Ai—the hill of Ai.

"Where's the bull?" demanded Medb.

"You are not to have him except by cunning or force," said Fergus, and told the whole story without quibble.

"No need for fancy speaking," cried Medb. "It is no secret that I would take the bull by weight of arms if it was not freely given. Spears, swords, shields and chariots! Assemble them! We go to war!"

"Gracious Queen," I said. "Permit me, although a stranger, to tell you now a story concerning cattle raiding from which you may draw what counsel you will. I am myself, as you know, returning from a war of many years' duration to my home in Ithaka. I was forced to blind Polyphemos, the one-eyed son of Poseidon, and that great lord of the sea and earthquakes has prevented my return for many years."

"His name is Manannan, not Poseidon," said Medb. "We know where he lives and we will settle his business for him as soon as we have the Brown Bull of Cuailnge to pleasure himself among our patient cows. No doubt about that. You have but to fight with us, your natural allies. Then home to Ithaka, if you wish, with no Manannan to vex you."

Inwardly I quaked at such blasphemy and irreverence for the gods. "Great Queen," I said, "no good can come from such lack of respect for the great god of the seas and oceans."

"Fiddle-dee-dee," said Medb. "What good has Manannan ever done us but assault our coasts and drown our sailors and fisherfolk? When the gods war with men, let the gods look out. They must be taught their manners. But if you have a story to tell, which I presume will be a long one, come lie on the bed beside me. There you will be more comfortable—and if I weary of the tale, I will have something else to contemplate."

Seeing her devotion to Hermes, I sent a quick prayer to that messenger of the gods and exalter of sexual pleasures that he befriend me against the wrath of Poseidon, brother to great Zeus himself.

Nothing was to be done but to settle myself on the queen's bed as far from her as I might and tell my tale. Ailill went off. The thought of war aroused him. He was naturally lazy, but he loved a battle, as indeed do all these Celts. He went to look over his weapon hoard and his war chariots, and to plan the route to Ulster with Fergus Mac Roth.

"Come closer," said Medb. "I am a little hard of hearing

in that ear. If you tire of your tale, or your mind wanders to other thoughts, I shall not be offended."

No tale was ever told in such circumstances. Yet I went on with it. Who despairs of success has lost the battle before a blow is struck.

"It happened that on my way homeward from Troy in my dark-hulled ship I came upon an island where lived a daughter of the sun. The land was strange to me. Some god unknown, to whom I now give open thanks, conned my ship safely into a little cove with a rocky headland to the northward, warding off the night wind."

"What was the name of this daughter of the sun?" asked Medb.

"Deirdre Connor," I replied. "No. That was not her name. It was Circe."

"I mix up their names myself often enough," said Medb. "Come closer. I feel a little cold. It would be a comfort if you would throw a strong leg over me."

"Great and beautiful Queen," I said, "why not save yourself for others better than I? Why expend your love on what may after all prove inferior?"

"There may be something in that," said Medb, "though it is not often I have a valiant Greek in my bed. Also I have plenty of love to spare. But what happened between the two of you? Tell me quickly. You went immediately to the bedchamber. That I know."

> *"Not so," I said. "Reflect, thou green-eyed*
> *Queen of Connaught,*
> *Mistress of ten thousand stiffened spears,*
> *How the apple quickly seized and eaten*
> *Gives but a bee's bite of the pleasure*
> *That same fruit could bring if taken only*
> *After much longing and painful plans.*

Circe certainly I loved
Through many a perfumed night of summer
When soft airs, spice laden, caressed us
Gently on that bed of silk.
Music also, of flute and lyre, that fills the mind
With deep content, like a sail
Full blown in a home-bound wind
Swelled our longing until
O'ershadowing her, she cradled in my
Sea-strong arms,
We merged, as one wave overtakes the other
Two into one. . . ."

"Did she wiggle?" asked Medb. "I like to wiggle."

"Quiet as hill shadow she lay,
Welcoming the life-giving sun."

"I'll try it," said Medb. "But I'll probably wiggle. It's hard for me to keep still. Go on with your tale."

"It came time for me to leave Circe, homeward bound to Ithaka," I said. "So once more I provisioned my great hollow ship, the enchantress helping me in every way. And she gave me many warnings of the dire perils that lay ahead and how they might be avoided.

"Here is one warning Circe gave me in which you may find counsel for yourself.

'All perils passed, Trinakria Island will loom
All green and gold upon your portside bow.
Here graze in knee-deep, dewy grass
The gleaming Cattle of the Sun.
No kindly bay or cove shall you seek
Upon that pleasant coast. Or if by chance
You make a landing there, raid not those sleek beeves;
Touch no one of them. They are the Sun God's pets.

None will survive who touch his grazing kine
But be destroyed, ship and men,
Lost to life and the warm sun
Forever. . . .'

"That, Great Queen, was the warning of the goddess who never spoke any word but truth to me. Reflect, then, that though Ulster is not Trinakria, this great bull of Cuailnge also may be one of the herd of the Sun God. Certainly you who keep many herds know how a bull will stray—yes, and even swim across the sea from land to land. The cows lie quiet, patient under the flies. But bulls will venture. The kine of Helios the Sun God are immortal. No feat for such an immortal bull to swim from land to land, and finding good grazing in this distant island and fine herds to service, linger a while.

"Reflect, I beg you. My own men, first persuading me to land upon that island, overtired after many perils, raided the cattle as you propose to do. Great waves pinned us to that accursed cove. Food ran out and seamen, eating leaves and grasses, cannot forever live among such sleek fat cows. Better, they said, to face the anger of the god Helios and be drowned at sea, or be killed by the thunderbolts of Zeus, than to die of starvation with food in plenty quietly grazing before them.

"In short, they killed the cattle, and although they made fat offerings to Zeus and to Helios himself, they were all destroyed when at last we manned our sun-warped oars, and put again to sea.

"Thunderbolts launched by Zeus split and fired my stout ship. Great waves rolled over her and drowned all. Only I survived. I beg you to leave the great bull of Cuailnge alone lest he also prove a pet of the Sun God."

"You are entirely wrong about that great bull of Cuailnge now grazing on the lands of the oaken farmer," said Medb.

"Let me say too that your men who raided the cattle of Helios and ate them were in my judgment right. Why should not starving men raid fat herds of cattle while they still have strength? That is the right thing to do, for it seems to me they would have died anyway. As to that great bull, I starve for it just as painfully as your men starved on that lush island. Like them, I will have the bull or die of longing for it. So better to have the bull and if some god whom I do not know is annoyed by the raid, then let him face me and I will face him. You will never find me quail before the gods. I have often prayed that the stronger among them would come to my bed, but not one has appeared yet.

"However, to ease your mind, I will tell you about that fine brown bull that I mean to have, if he costs me twenty thousand lives. It is true that the splendid creature is divine, as is the white bull of my lazy husband.

"Here is the story:

"There were two gods of the underworld, one in Connaught and one in Munster in the north. Each had a pigkeeper for their great herds of boars and sows. The name of the pigkeeper of the god of the underworld of Munster was Bristle and the name of the pigkeeper of the god of the underworld of Connaught was Grunt.

"They were close friends. One year one would drive his pigs to the other's feeding grounds and the herds would mix and the two would talk together. The next year it was turnabout.

"Friendship does not sit easy on common people, as you must know who have traveled so far. Soon, seeing how close Grunt and Bristle were, drinking wine together, eating together, wrestling together and sharing the same women, the common people started to sow an enmity between them.

" 'Grunt has more magic than Bristle,' they said.

"Or, 'Bristle has more magic than Grunt.'

"The two knew what was being said. 'We'll try it,' said Grunt. So he put a spell on his friend's swine so that, however much they ate, they didn't fatten.

" 'Good enough,' said Bristle. 'The west wind seems strong till the east wind blows.' He put the same spell on Grunt's pigs and they didn't fatten either.

"Then they changed themselves into cows and quarreled for a year in Munster and a year in Connaught. Talon and Wing they called themselves. Then they changed themselves into sea monsters, and their names were Whale and Seabeast. Then they changed themselves into warriors and fought bloodily, and their names then were Point and Edge.

"Then they became misty phantoms swirling around each other, and at that time their names were Shadow and Shield. Then they changed themselves into maggots, and nobody has a name for a maggot. Then one of them was swallowed by a cow of my husband's and from that swallowing Finnbennach, the white bull of Connaught, was born.

"The other was swallowed by a cow of Daire Mac Fiachna's and from that the Brown Bull of Cuailnge was born. No doubt they'd fight if they met again, and meet they will. Although they are divine, your god Helios had better not claim the Brown Bull of Cuailnge as his own, or he will find the united swords of Connaught and Ulster flashing in his eyes.

"Steward! Find a harper."

"What do you want a harper for at this time, great Queen?" I asked.

"What worked for that Greek enchantress Circe should work for me," said Medb.

It cannot be denied that she would not be turned aside from any purpose. When all was done, she leaped out of bed.

"Swords, shields, spears, chariots!" she cried. "We're going to war!"

CHAPTER

15

━━━━━━━━━━━━━━━━━━━━━━━━━

tHE ARMIES STARTED MASSING THE NEXT DAY. Through misty and storm-lashed defiles in the mountains, across wide plains and gloomy boglands, the warriors came in troops, each under their commander, answering the war summons of Medb.

As from every great house among the Achaeans, and from every modest croft as well, sturdy, strong-limbed lads had come for the assault on Troy, so now the warriors gathered for the assault on Ulster. It was not a thousand ships they launched, but a thousand chariots. The great plain of Ai around Cruachan was blue with the smoke of campfires from dawn to dusk. Horses and men crowded every foot of ground from Cruachan to the Sinann River. When the horses were led each evening to that sweet-flowing water to drink, you could have walked a mile across their massed backs. The charioteers drank first, to test the purity of the water. Better a man turn sick and die than a horse. So they viewed the matter.

The hooves of that vast herd, moving to the drinking place on signal, naked, muscled men upon their backs, shouting, jeering, laughing, mocking at each other, shook the ground as thunder shakes the earth under the wrath of Poseidon. At the drinking place they were out of sight of Cruachan beyond a slight rise of the ground. Yet we knew the moment they started to return, for the ground trembled under their feet and the walls of the fortress shook as in an earthquake.

Hour by hour, new bodies of men arrived on the crowded plain. Each troop under its commander was distinguished by the color of its cloaks and the style of hair dressing among the warriors. So it was among the Achaeans pouring down the craggy peaks to launch the dark ships against distant Troy.

The troop of Cet, brother of Ailill, had white cloaks striped in black, and their hair was tied in braids—one on each side of the head, and one down the back. They carried war axes. The troop of Murcorb, brother also of Ailill, had cloaks of black with white right-handed spirals following the path of the sun, and carried mighty spears. Their hair was tied in a knot on the top of their heads, and they wore no helmets.

The troop of Cormac, son of Conchobor, who had led his warriors to Ulster after the disgrace of Derdriu's betrayal, wore purple cloaks and, under this, red embroidered tunics with hoods on them. These tunics reached to their feet. They were spearmen all, each having a broad-bladed spear and a shield with the edges in half-moons. A mighty host. All fought naked in single combat or in general battle, their shields their only defense, for that is the custom among these Celts. They thought no more of death than of losing a tooth to an iron-fisted blow, which they often suddenly gave each other in pure sport.

More even than the Achaeans, they lived with their gods around them, always aware of signs and omens. A tree felled by a windstorm could stop their army for a day. A swan flying down the wind might send them helter-skelter back to where they started from. Such was the effect of divine signs upon them.

They rebelled only against Poseidon, whom they called Manannan. When they came to any body of water, stormy or quiet, in they went with their spears, thrusting here and there lest that god should have taken refuge from them in it. I offered secret prayers nightly that I would not be judged as taking part in these outrages.

For two weeks the army assembled, and then lingered two weeks more while the druids and soothsayers awaited a sign. Mountains of forage had to be brought in to feed the horses. A herd of pigs or of sheep was slaughtered each day to feed the warriors. The whole plain was soon piled thick with horse droppings, and the skulls and bones of the animals devoured. Rain fell, since it was now the change of the year, and made a muddy mixture of dung, mud and bones. Flies soon outnumbered the warriors, their buzzing to be heard even above the clanging of the sword- and spearmakers' hammers and the restless thunder of the horses' hooves.

"Let's move," said Fergus one morning, slapping the flies off a hunk of roast pork he was about to eat.

A druid passing by heard him. He came from Ath Luain. "First a sign," said the druid.

"Here it is," said Fergus, and threw his spear through him.

"You are right," said Medb. "Sound the trumpets. Off we go. Many a curse I'll earn from those who leave lovers and women behind them. It is Ailill's fault. He should never have vexed me by saying in bed that it was fortunate for a woman to marry a wealthy man. My blood boils even now at the thought."

"A war over so small a matter?" I ventured.

"Small?" she shouted, pounding the ground with the haft of her spear. "I'd kill all of Ulster for the half of it."

The war trumpets were sounded—great clattering, vile instruments like a thousand sticks being rattled against a mile of palings—and in a whirlwind of movement all sought chariots and charioteers and raced for the river.

"Goad those beasts," screamed Medb to her charioteer. "They must breast the water first. I'll take no spray from chariots ahead."

"First a sun-wise circle for a safe return," cried the charioteer. Right-handed he spun the horses, the chariot pivoting on one enormous wheel so fast as to dig a hole to its axle. Then off, straight through the mob ahead, Medb, bare-breasted, beating horses and chariots aside with her spear to be first to the river. So she was. Right after her at full speed thundered a thousand chariots, the flying hooves and whirling wheels flinging the water in shining walls a hundred feet into the air, such was the fury and the speed with which those leather-armored carriages of war assaulted the river. Indeed, where they crossed, the Sinann was dry for a while, the water at the place of crossing having been flung upstream or down, or on the land itself.

"So much for Manannan," cried Medb. "I'll stream his guts on my chariot pole yet. Uliseacht, see you sleep with me tonight."

"Glorious Queen," I said, "you have at your back thousands of warriors, many stronger than I and equally strange. . . ."

"Bring a harper," she added.

Truly no siren could have been more demanding than the Queen of Connaught.

Across the Sinann we came upon a woman seated alone in the path of the army. She wore a speckled cloak fastened close over her breasts with a gold pin, and her hair flowed over a hood of scarlet.

She looked with steady eyes at the queen.

"Who are you?" demanded Medb.

"Fedelm my name; the poetess, of Connaught."

"Where have you come from?"

"Alba, the place of verse and arms and visions."

"Have you the Light of Foresight?"

"None better."

"Look well at my army. Tell its fate."

She looked.

"Out with it," said the queen. "Who lives? Who dies?"

"I see scarlet. I see blood," said Fedelm.

"We're not going to a picnic," said Medb. "Wounds, blood, split bones, splattered brains—that's part of the business. What the result?"

> *"The golden-haired Hound*
> *Of Chulainn the Smith—*
> *Him I see. Water behind him,*
> *Blood before him.*
> *Heads heaped high,*
> *An army crimsoned*
> *By his hand.*
> *Thick the slaughter*
> *His chariot wheels scream*
> *At the screaming men*
> *Beneath their rims.*
> *Ravens feasting,*
> *Women wailing,*
> *Bodies torn,*
> *This I see.*
> *Bloody the hands of*
> *The Forge-Hound*
> *Cúchulainn,*
> *Guardian of Ulster,*
> *Keeper of the Ford."*

"We could start again tomorrow," suggested Ailill thoughtfully.

"Fiddle-dee-dee," said Medb. "Forward! I'll break the back of that hound over my own fine knee!"

Away she dashed. A thousand chariots dashed after her.

CHAPTER

16

ONWARD THE GREAT ARMY THUNDERED EAST BY south, a dark tide flowing over marshy bog, emerald plain and misty mountain. From the center it was impossible, even standing on the chariot rim, to see the right wing or the left wing or the rearguard—such was the expanse of that multitude of warriors.

"Uliseacht," cried Medb, "turn right about with me and we will make a circuit of the army."

"Onward," cried Fergus. "No holding back. I see ravens gathering."

"Two spear lengths ahead of you I will be, Fergus Mac Roth, when we sight the warriors of Ulster, awaiting death," cried Medb. "Meanwhile I go to see who presses forward, who lags, who claims lame horses, who thinks of his woman's warm arms and spares the goad. Uliseacht, follow."

Around her chariot spun, streaming ahead of the army toward the distant right wing. After her I followed, clods of earth flinging into my chariot car from the flying hooves ahead. Fifteen miles was the circuit of the army, which took us two hours of hard goading, with never a stop to make. One glance the queen gave at each troop, and could tell with that glance who lagged and who pressed, who was eager and who fainthearted.

Back she came, and called a halt while she conferred with Fergus. "It would be wise to send back the warriors of Galeoin of Leinster," she said.

"What madness has you now?" cried Fergus. "Better fighting men you will not find in Connaught. A pleasure to die among such men, lusting like wild boars for battle."

"That's it," said the queen. "They are ahead of everybody. They will do great deeds and claim every triumph for themselves."

"What of that?" said Ailill. "They are fighting on our side."

"They have to leave," said Medb. "I won't abide anyone claiming greater spirit than myself. Besides, they are dangerous. When we have taken the bull, they will attack us and seize our kingdom."

"Was there ever a creature more stupid than a woman?" cried Ailill. "Truly the cow can't lead the herd."

"Listen well to me," said Fergus. "You do not order fighting warriors like those of Galeoin to return home once summoned to war. They would not obey."

"Then we must kill them all," said Medb. "I won't have them with me."

"That is truly a woman's way of thinking," said Fergus. "Pure wickedness. These men are our friends. You will kill them over my dead body and those of the men of Ulster with you."

"That might be done," said Medb. "Half the host is mine. We could decide that now."

"Ask that Greek warrior," said Ailill. "There may be some way between ordering them home and killing them."

"What does he know of such matters?" demanded Medb.

"He has been in many wars," said Ailill. "What happens once has happened before. The first crane you see flying is not the first crane to fly."

"Well," said Medb, "I think we should kill them. But let Uliseacht speak."

"Why turn aside such willing swords?" I said. "The day might come when three such men may hold the line against the red hedge of spears. Divide them instead. Scatter them through the army. Then you will have the use of them and they cannot boast that it was they alone who did this thing or that thing."

"Good advice," said Fergus. "But how do you get them to split up?"

"That is easily done," I replied. "You have but to tell them that they are such good soldiers that you wish to divide them among the host so that the rest may catch their zeal and follow their example."

"The worm tunnels through the tree that split the bear's skull," said Ailill. "It is no wonder to me, Uliseacht, that you have survived so many perils."

It was done, but that did not stop the men of Galeoin from distinguishing themselves. A little later that vast horde came on a plain with a herd of wild deer in the center. They appeared no bigger than rabbits when first seen, so great was the distance. The host encircled the herd and slaughtered them all. There were one hundred and sixty deer; one hundred and twenty of them were killed by the warriors of Galeoin, the others by the rest of the army.

That evening the rain stopped and the air became suddenly so cold that in a minute the whole host was enveloped in the misty breath of men and horses. Dark clouds streamed over the sky from the north and with them came wind seething, moaning and whistling over that miserable plain where we had killed the deer, whose bloody hides, draped over the sides of the chariots, were soon frozen stiff.

Snow fell in tiny beads to sting our faces like fire. Any sea rover would now have quickly found the lee of some island to shelter against this divine wrath. But that impious army made no move toward the distant mountains where an easing of the storm might be sought. Indifferent, they settled down by their chariots, swords, spears, shields and axes to hand, the horses hobbled in pairs nearby, as the mighty wind whistled over them, scattering the embers of the fires.

All night the wind blew and the snow fell faster. Soon the snow was piled in drifts about the chariots, burying them to their axles. No offering was made to any god; no inner meat or thigh bone of a single deer burned in sacrifice.

Here certainly was a warning against taking the divine bull of Cuailnge. So I offered a prayer to the god who undoubtedly had sent this storm.

With wind-numbed hands I lit a small fire under the car of my chariot and, taking some of the inner meats of the deer which I had put aside for this purpose, I roasted them on it. Then I said this prayer to Helios.

Holy Father of life-giving light
Whose lovely daughter, rosy-fingered Dawn,
Delight of the gods, never visited
These dark and rain-lashed lands,
Hear the cry of mortal Ulysses
He who in far Trinakria alone of all his crew
Touched not your sleek and grazing cattle
But starving, shipwrecked, drifted on the sea
To the foul suck hole Charybdis,
Obedient to your will.

You cannot grumble at such loyalty
Nor turn aside the prayer of one
So faithful to his word. Truly no god
Blazing with warmth and light could
Turn a dark countenance upon
Such a man. Therefore, I plead,
Take notice that it is no plan of mine
To wrest your sacred far-ranging bull
From the sweet grasslands and pretty heifers
Of Cuailnge. Swept as in a storm
Rudderless, my mast gone overboard
And ox-hide backstays severed through,
I am carried on this impious raid.
Save me, then, who never thought,
Not for one moment, to raise a hand
Against your fine kine. . . .
Lord of all the life-giving light,
Deliver me. . . .

When this prayer was said, the fire blazed up and died: a happy omen. Not a spark remained, but only a vestige of smoke from the burned meats. The cold in a moment seeped deeper into my bones, and through the murk beyond the chariot pole, I saw a light approach, wavering, dimming, weaving here and there.

Then, beside the chariot stood a slim, cloaked figure, one hand held toward me, and in its palm a soft ball of light.

"Circe," I cried.

"I am Fedelm," she answered. "Come, Wandering Man. You shall not sleep with this freezing host tonight, but in my own warm and welcoming arms." So speaking, she turned and I followed her swiftly through that snow-covered mass of men, horses and chariots, with here and there the ears of a horse, the pole of a chariot or the point of a spear thrust above the mantle of snow.

CHAPTER

17

S OME DISTANCE OFF THERE WAS A FOREST OF YEW
and pine in a valley between the mountains. We entered the shelter of its boughs, and the howling wind
was silenced and the driving snow held back. Nothing
of storm or winter was to be seen under the fragrant
trees, except here and there a gleam of snow on the dark forest
floor. The goddess led me up a little tree-pillared hill with,
at its foot, the diamond flash of a rivulet. There, snug against
a giant yew, was a cave and, inside, a bed of boughs, covered
with the thick-furred skins of bears.

The place was lit, and to the scent of pine was added that
of the wild bluebell and the violet.

"We need no lute players," said the lovely goddess with a smile. "The stream provides soft music for our love."

She let fall one of the shoulder straps of her tunic to reveal one golden, rounded breast. "It is a long time since I have held you in my arms," she said.

Yet I held back, fearing some trap.

"Why should you fear me, Ulysses?" she asked. "Surely you know it is impious to refuse the gifts of the gods and dangerous to keep them waiting. Have I shown you any ill-feeling in bringing you here away from that impious army marching toward an ocean of blood?"

"Truly, no," I replied. "Yet, Goddess, tell me plainly; have you some stratagem in mind by which to enslave me, or am I here only that I may receive the delight of your kisses and embraces? Will you swear that you intend me no harm and will you promise to befriend me who am on so long a journey to my home? I am no boy, as you know, but a seasoned, well-trained traveler used to wiles and tricks."

Then the goddess smiled and said, "It is your cunning, Ulysses, as well as your courage that makes me love you and invite you here. Of all that host, you are the wisest and most experienced. Only you can truly match wits with the gods. But put aside your fears. No harm will come to you, I promise, and certainly I will befriend you and warn you of many hazards that lie in your path, you who have been lost for so long."

Then she dropped her tunic and paused for one moment naked before me. Into the bearskins then she slipped, leaving only her lovely head and one arm exposed. Quickly I shed helmet, boots and war gear and followed her into that soft bed of love. So, while the river tinkled its gentle song and the air was sweet with the scent of wild flowers, we loved each other until at last, entwined and satisfied, we fell asleep.

When I awoke, Fedelm was sitting by the side of the bed.

((134   ))

"It is time now to talk of the perils that await you, if you do not want to leave your head in Conchobor's gory hall," she said.

"Drink this and do not fear it. It will refresh you now that you have awakened." She gave me a chalice of gold, the amethysts with which it was studded matching the rich wine within. When I had drunk she said, "It is dangerous for you to be traveling with the host of Medb and Ailill. There is but one man to guard all of Ulster because of the curse laid on Conchobor's warriors when he raced his stallions against the woman Macha. Be warned. That one guardian is Cúchulainn, the Hound of the Smith. Soon, because of him, there will be among Medb's warriors as many smashed skulls and headless bodies, meat for the birds, as if all Conchobor's eager men had been loosed upon them. To their doom they march."

"How can one man wreak such havoc among a host as mighty as that which follows Medb?" I asked. "There is not a man among them who is not eager for slaughter. You have seen how they press forward in their chariots, a vast flood sweeping over the plains and mountains of this darkened land. Any one of them is certainly a match for this Cúchulainn who, as I remember him, has done nothing but splash the brains of a fierce dog against the granite walls of Chulainn's fort—a feat hardly to be noted among fighting men."

"No warrior in all the world—not among any of the nations or tribes whom the gods have put on the life-giving earth —ever equaled or will equal that Smith's Hound—Cúchulainn," the goddess replied. "Achilles would be no match for him, nor Hector, nor Agamemnon. As for yourself, better not make the trial if you want to see your home in Ithaka again. Be warned then. Do not be tricked by Medb into such a challenge, for if you are, only Poseidon himself, whom you have grievously offended by putting out the eye of the Cyclops, can aid you."

At these words my heart quaked. Miserable indeed my fate if, at the end of all my voyagings, I should be killed in a war with which I had no concern, killed like a rabbit which, having eluded hounds, wolves and foxes, is brained by the stone of a careless boy.

I wept at the thought of such a fate, and clasped the knees of the goddess and begged her to advise me how to escape this peril.

"Do not be so cast down, Ulysses," she said. "You who have faced man-eating Scylla and that foul vomit of the ocean, Charybdis, you who have escaped the blood-gorging horde of Antiphates. You are not the man to fall unwittingly to Cúchulainn's harpoon-pronged belly spear or his lightning swift sword or deadly sling. Warned, you will certainly find some subtle way to avoid the challenge. But let me tell you something of this Death Hound's feats, that you may better know how to handle him if you should find him in your way.

"First, as I have said, there is no one in the world superior to him in weapons, for he was trained as a lad by Scáthach, the war goddess, on her island home off Alba. To reach that island you must cross a bridge. But as soon as you set your foot on one end of the bridge, the other end rises straight up in the air, so that the island may not be reached. Yet Cúchulainn, by a mighty leap, reached the middle of the bridge and with another jumped from there to the island. Such his skill and strength. On the island he met Scáthach's daughter Uathach.

" 'Come lie with me,' he said. 'I've seed to sow, ripe and ready.' He seized her, but she cried out and the mighty champion of the war goddess, Cochar Cruibne, rushed at him, sword flashing, shield trembling with wrath. Cúchulainn parried his thrust, left-handed, and cut off his head.

" 'Yours is the seed for me,' said the girl. 'But first you must put your sword between my mother's breasts and make her promise you thoroughness in training, a dowry for your marriage and tidings of the future.'

" 'Which sword will serve best?' asked Cúchulainn.

" 'The one at your waist,' said the daughter.

"So Cúchulainn rushed at Scáthach with a naked sword and got those three promises from her, and received the best training in weapons ever given to mortal man. So good was that training that he met the war goddess Aife, archenemy of Scáthach, in single combat. By a trick, he distracted her attention, and, his sword being broken to a nub, rushed at her, seized her by the breasts, flung her over his back and brought her back screaming to Scáthach.

"There, threatening to kill her, he got three further promises from her—that she would forget her hatred of Scáthach, that she would couple with him all that night and that she would bear him a son. All three promises were fulfilled.

"Now I complete my short account. Listen carefully, Wandering Man. Cúchulainn is no ordinary mortal. When he is seized by the battle fury, one eye recedes in his head until it is no bigger than the hole in a small needle, and the other becomes as big as a goblet and rolls about in its socket, bloodshot and blood-seeking. His lips roll back until through his bared, gnashing teeth you may see his gullet. From the top of his head, tall as the mast of your far-voyaging ship, a spout of dark blood rises in the air. Be warned by that description, Wanderer."

These words set my heart quaking lest I be doomed to leave my bones on this dark island, far from sunny Ithaka. "Goddess, I thank you that you have taken pity on me and shown me so many signs of your regard for me. I would be ungrateful indeed if I did not follow your advice in every detail. I will seek a way to leave the host of Medb, though it will not be easy. I beg you put whatever opportunities you can in my way, for if I sneak off, they will hunt me down.

"But if I succeed in deserting them, Fergus and Dubthach and every warrior on the side of that fierce queen will vow to cut off my head. Therefore I plead with you that you will not forget me but continue to extend to me your aid."

The goddess said not a word but only smiled and pointed to the mouth of the cave. Shroud-colored Dawn was graying the sky. I turned to say one more word of heartfelt thanks to Fedelm, but found the cave empty, nor any sign of the bed on which we had lain together in delight.

Boots, shirt, armor and helmet then I put on, and returned to the cold camp of Medb.

CHAPTER

18

n OT A MORSEL OF FOOD DID THAT RECKLESS ARMY
of Medb have to eat the next day. Hungry and grum-
bling, they struggled out of their beds of snow to
find that the baggage cars and packhorses were
snowed in far to the rear. Not a scrap of deer meat
had they saved from the slaughtered herd, such was their lack
of foresight.

The life-giving sun, Helios, did not show himself that day.
No. Helios hid himself from their unworthy eyes behind a
curtain of dark cloud. The wind whistled and whimpered over
the snow. The men's breath froze on their beards, a white O

of frost about their mouths. Noses were blue and knuckles too, and ears red. Icicles of saliva hung from the lower lips of the horses and they also had a frozen powdering of breath rimming their nostrils.

Yet these tough warriors were not downcast by their plight, but shaking the snow from themselves, flung the drifts away from their chariots and unburied their steeds and prepared to plunge forward against Ulster again.

"Who did you find to keep you warm last night?" asked Fergus when he caught sight of me. "Medb was roaring for you, and her harper froze two of his fingers, playing love tunes while she waited. I'd give her a wide berth if I were you. That woman does not like to be disappointed in anything. See how she flings this whole army at Ulster for a bull."

"She might have had the bull without effort but for your sly tongue, Fergus Mac Roth," I replied.

"True indeed," said Fergus. "Now see how you can use your sly tongue to escape from her unrequited desire."

Dubthach, the Dark One, was stropping his bronze sword on a honing stone nearby. He also was among those who had left Ulster over the betrayal of Derdriu of the Sorrows and the Sons of Uisliu.

"I had her last night," he said. "But first I killed that harper. Better music before bed is sword on bone than tinkling strings. Tonight, if I can first kill a man in fierce combat to get my vigor up, I shall have her again." He glanced at me with hard eyes. "Perhaps there is some reason why you and I should fight, Uliseacht," he said. "Your tracks in the snow, which I have followed, led from the camp toward the Ulster boundary. Is it possible that you sent warning of our coming?"

"To what purpose?" I asked. "Is it of any weight to me who wins or who loses in this combat in which I have no part?"

"A promise of rich acres in Ulster to a wandering man might give him purpose," said Dubthach, testing the edge of his blade on his thumb. "On the other hand, if you are innocent, you have a right to resent by weapon the inferences I have made before others against you."

A javelin lay close to hand. It was no feat to swiftly throw it at Dubthach's stout shield. Clean through, haft and all it went, such was the anger of my throw, cutting as well its neat path along Dubthach's arm, from which the blood oozed.

"Bring your father and your brothers and your sons to aid you if you would meet a veteran of the Trojan horse," I said. "You will have need of them."

"That we will see," said Dubthach. "That was a good cast, but I can make a better."

It was no javelin, but his keen-edged sword he threw. Long ago, from my father Laertes, I had learned the flying sword feat, and so caught it by the hilt, ducking aside from the circling blade.

"That was well done," said Dubthach. "Only Cúchulainn and Fergus have mastered that trick."

"Take back the sword," I said. "Let us end this silly quarrel. I slept last night in a cave in that warm forest rather than under the frozen wheels of the war chariot. Hence my footsteps."

Fergus and Dubthach looked slyly at each other.

"I would like to see that cave," said Fergus.

"If our way leads through that forest, you shall see it," I replied. "Also the great yew which marks its entrance."

"We do not go through the forest, but southward and eastward," said Fergus.

Again that look between them, which set me thinking, though Dubthach now covered the wound on his arm with snow to stanch the bleeding. Neither wine nor oil will these barbarous fighters pour on their wounds, but only such things as snow or the ashes of hazel wood, or the juice of the berries of mistletoe, which they hold will cure every condition. Had not that very juice restored vigor to Cathbad? I had some vague memories, a glimpse of something solid soon lost in sea fog, of such a happening.

Those glances between Fergus and Dubthach warned me of some conspiracy between them. Also it was strange that Dubthach had sought a quarrel with me and it was no accident that he was there with Fergus that morning. What plot, I asked myself, were they hatching against me? It is the fool who, walking a dangerous road, ignores the slightest sign. His sudden end is no real cause for lamentation, since he brought it on himself through carelessness.

Yet, one sign on the road of hazard, examined alone, might be meaningless unless put together with others. Reflecting on this, I thought of two things which were curious about the march of that great army of Medb's on Ulster.

The first was that, despite all his zeal, Fergus, who was the one really in command despite Medb's bluster, did not take the army on a direct route to Ulster. Not eastward toward the rising sun we went, but southeast, wasting days despite his show of zeal. Again, though an experienced warrior, he had camped on that open plain in a coming storm, when forest and mountains nearby offered shelter from the biting winds and flying snow. That camp delayed the army further, for to uncover horses and chariots and render the frozen traces and reins and snaffles supple once more was the work of a morning. Fergus, then, showed outward zeal, but secretly delayed.

Then also there were Dubthach's surprising charges, that I had during the night gone toward Ulster. Experience itself has taught me that it is of their own faults and sins that men accuse each other. Treachery is the first cry of the traitor. So I decided that Fergus, former King of Ulster, had himself sent word to his old comrades and subjects that the army of Connaught was marching on their frontier.

Now I saw my own danger plainly. It would be I, a stranger

whose loyalties were unknown, who would be first accused of sending a warning to Ulster. While I was thinking all this over Medb sent for me.

"The harper is killed, and all your fault," she said when she caught sight of me. "I had to take Dubthach to bed to keep me warm, and he had no use for sweet music. What delayed you?"

"Great Queen, that is a small matter," I said. "I was delayed going out in the icy snow and wind to scout about the camp and see all was well. In the dark I lost my way, having no campfires nor even a friendly star to guide me back."

"You were a fool to go out then," she said. "Help me bind this chariot pole. That hulking stallion leaned on it, and, frozen, it snapped under his weight."

She was wrapping a length of oxhide around the break, pulling it tight with her white teeth.

"I like your strong arms, Uliseacht," she said as I helped her. "But there is not a harper in the camp who can sweeten our bed tonight, for they are all afraid and claim that in the cold their strings break so they cannot play."

"There are things more important than that to think about," I said.

"Tell me one."

"This war—this cattle raid."

"You have me there. What of it?"

"Why have we so much southing in our course when our goal lies due east?" I asked. "It is no headwind that we tack against, board on board. There is nothing to prevent steering straight east for the Ulster border."

"There's something in that," she said.

"Also why did we lie out here in the open plain last night, exposed to wind and snow until all were buried in it, when an hour's march would have taken us to the shelter of the forest or those northern hills?"

"Easily answered," she said. "To toughen the men."

"They're tough enough," I said. "A night and a day in the snow would tire them, not season them."

"That's Fergus's doing," she said, pulling the last knot tight with her tough teeth.

"It is, and Fergus is an Ulsterman."

"Bring him here," said the queen. "He's a stupid man, like all men."

I found Fergus again among the Ulster troops. "The queen wants you," I said. "On your way to her you would be well advised to think of a reason why the army does not march directly to Ulster, and why you camped out here and caused half a day's delay."

"No need to think," said Fergus. "I'll soon tell her the reason."

"Out with it," said the queen. "No dilly-dallying. Why do we take this roundabout course to Ulster and why did you let the army get bogged down in this swirling snow? You're in command. What is your reason?"

"My reason is to delay the assault until the men of Ulster are prepared for us," said Fergus.

"A fine trick," said the queen. "What good will that do the men of Connaught?"

"None at all," said Fergus boldly. "But you would not expect me to descend secretly with a horde like this behind me on my own countrymen."

"Fair enough," said the queen. "But Ulster can rally her warriors in half a day. Why delay longer?"

"Ulster cannot rally her warriors for four days and five nights, or for five days and four nights," said Fergus.

"And why not?"

"Because of the curse."

"What curse?" demanded Medb, for the story had been kept from her.

((144   ))

"The curse of Macha. For when she spilled first her two children and then her guts before Conchobor's palace, racing against his fine stallions, she put this curse on the men of Ulster, that in time of peril all her warriors would endure the pangs of childbirth for four days and five nights or five days and four nights, according to when the peril was made known to them. They are rolling and groaning and shouting and cursing and calling for hot water and clean blankets and midwives at this very moment."

"Conchobor too?" asked the queen.

"Conchobor too."

"That is a sight I'd like to see. Who guards Ulster?"

"One man alone, Cúchulainn."

"And how old is he—I've scarcely heard the name," said Medb.

"Seventeen."

"Forward," roared the queen. "Forward. Bloody the goads. Kill any laggard that hangs back. I'll have that bull by the nose tomorrow."

CHAPTER

19

DAY LATER THE ARMY, NOW HURLING ITS DARK AND blood-seeking tide straight toward Ulster, reached a river, itself a tributary of the Boann, which name means the River of the Little Cow. This marked the Ulster border, but headstrong Medb had reached it at a place where, whatever their fury against water, the army could not cross, so deep did the river run.

In rushed the warriors despite the depth and the rush of the water, beating on the river in impious wrath against Manannan. That great god, whose real name is Poseidon, drowned a hundred of them and a hundred and fifty of their horses before they stopped.

"Find a ford," cried Medb. "We'll crash through him where his strength is thinnest. The best stroke is under the armpit or into the groin, and no one calls that shameful."

Fergus wanted to send men from the Galeoin troop, now dispersed among the army, to find a ford. "They're the best soldiers we have," he said. "Let them do good work for us."

"Never," cried Medb. "I couldn't abide that constant boasting that would follow. They would tell all Ireland that, but for them, the army could never have got into Ulster."

"Would you fling away a sword lest it boast that its keen edge alone cut down your enemy?" demanded Fergus.

The matter was settled by sending the four sons of Urard Mac Anchinee out to look for a ford. Their names were Err and Innel and Foich and Fochlam. Err and Innel were warriors and their brothers Foich and Fochlam their charioteers. As with the Achaeans, the tie between warriors and charioteers is as close as that of brothers, so much does the life of one lie in the hands of the other.

Off the charioteers dashed, trampling flat the brown sedges by the river's side, the squeak and crackle of the frost beneath their terrible wheels mingling with the scream of the horses and the reckless shouts of the four fighting men.

"Should not scouts be more silent in spying out the land?" I asked.

"Queer fighting they do in your country," said Dubthach. "Does one man steal up on the other and bash in his head? Is that a glorious victory?"

"The greatest of weapons is a man's own mind," I said. "Throw that away, Dark Warrior, and you will soon have your beard scattered over your chest and your head on a pole. Let us see how loud the sons of Mac Anchinee shout on their return."

Those were words of foresight, and bore bitter fruit. The two chariots returned slowly that evening, the steeds bloodied and wild-eyed. In the cars were the hacked bodies of the four sons of Urard Mac Anchinee, headless, the thick blood making a jelly on the floor of the chariots and mingling with the brooches and rugs and cloaks which had been the treasures of the young warriors.

All gathered around those gory chariots and the wild-eyed horses.

"Well," said Medb, "it's plain they were outnumbered. The men of Ulster have recovered from their pangs and the whole army guards that ford. Here's the first birth—death itself—from their labor."

Sencha, the Old Warrior, white haired, thin faced, his beard, too, thinned at the ears, looked over the warriors in the cars.

"One champion's work alone lies before us," he said. "The same sword cut, left to right, lopped off each head. Level with the shoulders, through the thickest part of the neck, that sword went. Strong the arm that wielded it; quick the eye. This is Cúchulainn's work."

"A beardless boy?" cried Medb. "Fiddle-dee-dee. You've lost your wits."

"Beardless or bearded," said Fergus, "I know him well. With one thunder shout he killed three hundred men who stood between him and his bride, Emer, in the stout granite-walled fortress of her father Fogall Monach, the Cunning. He took arms when he was eight years of age. Cathbad foretold that whoever armed himself that day would be the most famous warrior in Ireland, full of glory, but would die young. Cúchulainn heard him and demanded arms of Conchobor to fulfill that prophecy, caring nothing for a long life but only for great deeds.

"Ofttimes I've seen his great scythe-wheeled chariot return after the day's sport, the stark heads of a dozen men hanging about the car. The Warped One. That is another name for him, for the fearsome appearance he takes in his battle fury. He's greater in arms than Leagaire Buadach, the Victorious, or Conall Cernach, or Celtchar Mac Uthidir. Many times when he was a baby I held him on my knee, and he would not leave off bawling until he had my great sword in his tiny fists."

"We'll soon see about that," said Medb. "Tomorrow I'll send a stout seasoned warrior to challenge him at that ford. He cannot refuse."

"You will not send me," said Fergus.

"You fear him?" cried Medb.

"I do not fear him," said Fergus. "But I love him. That is worse."

That night the Dark One was taken by a fit of foresight and cried out in his sleep that there were dead warriors on every side, hacked and headless, all the work of Cúchulainn. Hardly a man could sleep over Dubthach's terrible outcry, and nothing could be done to silence him.

Signs more ominous appeared next day, full of direct warning. A spancel hoop, that is, a hoop made of a branch for hobbling horses or leading cattle by the neck, was found lying on a stone with words carved in the bark in *Ogham*, the magic language of these people.

"Read the words for us, Fergus Mac Roth," said Medb.

"This is Cúchulainn's work," said Fergus. "The words say that no man must come further unless someone can make a hoop to match this one, with one hand, and cut of one branch. I'm excluded, for I know the feat and am a friend of Cúchulainn."

"No need to pay any attention to that," said Medb.

"Wrong again," said Fergus. "For to pass by without accepting the challenge will bring terrible vengeance as well as shame on the whole army. That is the rule of war."

"Let us go around through that forest then," said Ailill. "I don't care if we pass that hoop. One way is as good as another."

They went through the forest, but had to cut a road through the thick trees, delaying them further.

"We'd have been longer making a spancel hoop with one hand," said Ailill.

They came to a ford across the river. There in the middle of the splashy broad stream was a mighty four-forked branch. Stuck on each branch was a bloodstained head, gray in the winter light—the heads of the fierce sons of Mac Anchinee, kites and crows thick around them, squawking at their feast.

"It's a wonder that he could cut off the heads of four such fierce and willing fighting men," said Medb.

"No wonder in that," said Fergus. "The wonder lies in that he cut that branch, thick as a tree, with one stroke of his sword. Two men might take six blows apiece and not have it off."

"Clear it out of the way," said Medb.

"Easily said. Hard to be done," said Fergus.

He took a chariot and passed a hitch around the forked branch. He goaded the horses and they dashed forward. The car of the chariot was torn from the axle. The branch remained firmly set in the riverbed.

"It was with one hand that he set it in," said Fergus. "No hole was dug to receive it. We'll smash chariots for an hour before we have it out."

That proved to be true for, in all, such was the strength of Cúchulainn, fourteen chariots were broken before that branch, thick through as a man's body, was pulled out of the riverbed. When the deed was done, Fergus showed Medb the butt end.

"One stroke of the sword cut it," he said.

The next day Medb called Fraech Mac Fidaig to her

chariot. She gave him a piece of the loin of a pig to eat and a cup of purple wine to drink and a barley cake to eat.

"Fraech," she said, as he wiped the grease of the pig loin off his fingers, "it's a good thing you are cleaning your hands. Slippery fingers will be a handicap in the work I have picked out for you. There is a nuisance in my way and the way of the army called Cúchulainn. Perhaps you have heard of him. A boy warrior, that is all. Get rid of him for me and tonight I will have other things to offer you."

"I'll do that," said Fraech.

He went off with nine warriors. They were soon back again.

"What happened?" asked Medb. "Where's Fraech?"

"Drowned like a kitten," said one of the nine. "He found Cúchulainn by the river and challenged him. 'What style of fighting do you prefer?' asked Cúchulainn. 'Stripped naked in midstream, one hand only on each other's shoulder. A wrestling match,' said Fraech.

" 'Agreed,' said Cúchulainn. In a twinkling he had Fraech's head under the water, held between his ankles. He let him up when his face was purple.

" 'Say the word and I'll spare your life,' he said.

" 'That word I cannot say,' said Fraech, and so Cúchulainn drowned him. He'd be cold company for you this night."

"I'll find another," said Medb.

That night the rain fell so heavily that not one chariot could be seen from another, nor any campfire lit. The men slept in the chariot cars, with hides and cloaks and shields stretched over the top for miserable shelter.

Suddenly a volley of great stones was hurled into the camp. Chariots were smashed, men's skulls and chests crushed, and horses killed. The crashing of broken wheels, the screaming of men and beasts, the thunder of the rain on the ground and the humming of the boulders through the air filled the night. Some giant creature was attacking the army, hurling those death-dealing boulders. I thought of Polyphemos, the Cyclops son of Poseidon, whose eye I had burned out in his stinking cave.

> *That blinded ogre, in his darkened rage,*
> *Broke off a hill and heaved it after us.*
> *Ahead of our slim ship it plunged and raised*
> *A wave which washed her sternward to the shore.*
> *The longest boathook I quickly seized*
> *And fended the ship off while all my crew*
> *Bent groaning backs to bending creaking oars*
> *And with a racing stroke, pulled off.*
> *Then I shouted, safe at sea to taunt him,*
> *While my crew begged me to be silent.*
> *"Why bait the brute?" they cried. "He with one rock*
> *Will stave our planks and have us foundering."*
> *No heed I paid in my vaunting rage but cried,*
> *"Cyclops, if ever any ask*
> *Who put out that one light of your head*
> *Say it was Ulysses, Laertes' son from Ithaka,*
> *None other than that famed sea wanderer*
> *And raider of great cities, strongly held."*
> *And then he begged me to return, backwater,*
> *Come ashore. He'd treat me well and pray his father*
> *Poseidon, earthquake god and ruler of the seas,*
> *To be my friend. But I scorned him again,*
> *Said I'd kill him if I could and hurl*
> *Him into dark hell, where no help could reach*
> *His foul man-fattened carcass. . . .*

Then the Cyclops had prayed his father that if I was destined by the gods to return to my home in Ithaka, it would only be after dark years of wandering, all my men lost, and beset on every side by misfortune.

Was it Cyclops now, called Cúchulainn in this dreary land,

who bluntly sought my life again? Yet though men, horses and chariots were smashed around me, no boulder hit my own war cart and I believed that my prayer to Helios, disclaiming any part in this unholy raid to capture the sun god's bull, had been heard, and he was protecting me.

The storm of boulders continued all that night. One killed a squirrel perched on the rim of Medb's chariot and another her favorite dog, taking a morsel of roast pig from her hand. Yet not one had come near me or my chariot.

"Two hundred and ten men with smashed heads, fifty-three horses killed, a hundred and twenty lamed, and sixty chariots wrecked," said Fergus. "That's a great hand at throwing stones for you."

"If he doesn't stop it, we'll be stuck here until the Ulstermen give their last roar of agony and stand up ready to fight," said Ailill.

"Find out what he wants," said Medb. "Tell him I'll give him a portion of the Plain of Ai and six chariots and twenty-three servant girls and my own friendly thighs on top of it to seal the bargain if he'll just stop throwing boulders at the army."

"And keep a civil tongue in your head," said Ailill. "Don't go pulling the same boasting trick you did with Daire. Maybe you thought to keep my wife for yourself and that was the reason for angering Daire and starting this war. But I'll say who sleeps with her and who doesn't."

"Say what you will and I'll sleep with whom I will," said Medb. So they bickered with each other while I remained silent, pondering the true nature of this death-dealing warrior Cúchulainn against whom the goddess had warned me not to take arms.

CHAPTER

20

---

tHAT DAY FERGUS WENT OUT TO MEET CÚCHULAINN. With him went a proud warrior, Etarcomol, who was the son of Eda and Lethrenn and had been given in fosterage when he was a baby to Ailill and Medb.

He wore a black tunic with right-handed spirals in silver on it, and a three-horned helmet, with tusks of wild boar set around the rim, and he carried a red shield with a gold boss and a gleaming bronze sword with an emerald set in the end of the hilt, the emerald surrounded by twinkling diamonds.

He was one of the proudest warriors of the host, and

given to boasting. But it was because he was the foster son of Ailill and Medb that he was so splendidly equipped, and not because of his own strength in arms. The horses of his chariot were black, with a white blaze on their foreheads. The wheels of the chariot were of black bog oak, and there were five dried heads dangling by their hair from the side.

"Better not come," Fergus said to Etarcomol.

"You are not the one who says yes or no to me," said Etarcomol.

"True enough," said Fergus. "But if you come I fear that your pride and your insolence will cost you your life." Fergus turned to me. "You will come in my chariot," he said.

"I do not think that would be fitting," I replied. "Reflect that I am a stranger in this land and have no part in this quarrel. Many other warriors, of Ulster or of Connaught, can accompany you. Why take one who is at best only an on-looker?"

"It is true that you are a stranger and have no part in the quarrel," said Fergus craftily. "Yet that is the reason I choose you. For I am formerly King of Ulster, as you know, and Cúchulainn was in my care in his boyhood and is very dear to me and now defends my kingdom. Therefore it is better that someone who is not involved should come and report truthfully what takes place and what terms are agreed. If you are afraid to meet such a warrior as Cúchulainn—though I have tired of your boasting of great deeds in places no man knows of—you will be under my protection and no harm will come to you."

"It is imprudent to speak of fear to one such as I," I replied. "Yet I will confess that I see no reason to be struck down in a quarrel of no concern to me. There is no glory in that."

"Under my protection Cúchulainn will not harm you," said Fergus. "If you hold back, you will be disgraced before all the army. Do you flinch for all your brave words from even a sight of such a warrior?"

"As for my courage, you have seen some display of it in our battle against the Earth Men," I replied. "So I will come only to see who this Cúchulainn is and to bring back a true report of all that happens."

His charioteer whirled the great chariot about and I leaped in over the side. Off we thundered, through crisp snow, for in the early hours the rain had turned to sleet and the sleet to snow, over which was a frozen crust. Swathes of mist hung above the marshy ground here and there, to be parted by the furious assault of horses and chariots and then to close silently behind as we swept by. Three crooked-necked cranes glided past us—a good omen—and a red fox came out of a clump of bog willow and barked three times, sharp and clear in the winter air.

"A warning, that," shouted Fergus, and swung his weapon arm three times in a circle for protection.

"Of what is it a warning?" I asked.

"Cúchulainn is a Hound and the fox is a hound, and there is identity in the two. The fox warns not to anger Cúchulainn nor come too near his lair. There will be blood on the snow before there is blood in the west when the sun leaves us."

Through dead sedges and reeds the chariots crashed, thin panes of river ice crackling and squeaking under the rumbling wheels. Then the steeds were reined in, their breath rising in clouds in the cold air. A hundred paces off, on a little rise, stood another chariot, red as blood, the wheels gold, the sides stark with trophies of bear, boar and men. Two massive gray steeds, hobbled, muzzled the frozen ground, tearing it up with their hooves, to eat the dead grass—blade, stem, roots and all. No need to ask to whom that chariot belonged or who stood waiting beside it.

Fergus, sword, spear and shield put aside, moved toward

Cúchulainn. He was no monstrous brute now, dripping from his lips portions of human flesh and the whey of his sheep. Rather I saw a fine, golden-haired lad, broad shouldered, strong armed, his eyes gray and deep set under his brows. He looked just such a young warrior as had set out with me, sturdily pulling an oar in the long haul to distant Troy.

"My heart's welcome to you, Fergus," he said. "If the sun shone now I would give you half my share of its warmth; if it was the time of the salmon running, I would give you half the fish I take from the river; if water were found in a desert place, you should have my portion; and if your arm tired in battle, then I would stand and take your place."

"I thank you," said Fergus. "Your speech truly matches your deeds, Cúchulainn, and I would in return do these same services for you. But I have come to parley with you and ask on what terms you will agree to let the army of Medb move against Ulster and stop killing men and horses and smashing chariots with boulders throughout the night."

"Since you ask for terms, I will grant them, friend Fergus," said Cúchulainn. "Here is what must be done. Each day Medb must send a warrior to challenge me at this ford. While we are fighting, her army may move. When I have killed the warrior, then the army must stop where it is and do no plundering of houses nor take any cattle nor kill anyone nor take slaves."

"Those terms are agreed," said Fergus. "I will return quickly and tell Medb. These two are under my protection, so I ask your warrior's oath that you will do them no harm."

"The oath is given," said Cúchulainn, and Fergus went off, leaving me with the proud warrior Etarcomol, who was staring hard at the guardian of the ford.

"What are you staring at?" demanded Cúchulainn of him.

"You," said Etarcomol.

"One look is enough," said Cúchulainn. "What do you see?"

"No one to be afraid of. A mild young warrior without

((157   ))

terror or fury and with not a wound on his face nor a lost eye or finger to speak for him."

"You belittle me," said Cúchulainn. "Fergus protects you, so I will not be angered. Without him your bowels would be darkening on the gleaming snow at this moment."

"Threats kill no one," said Etarcomol. "I'll be the first of the men of Ireland to challenge you tomorrow."

"We'll see," said Cúchulainn.

Off went Etarcomol, scarcely giving me a moment to leap into the chariot with him, such was his fury.

"I can't wait for tomorrow," he shouted to the charioteer. "I have been insulted past bearing by that impudent boy. Wheel the horses about left-handed. Show him the left-hand boards of our chariot. Then he must fight." Such an insult, to turn a chariot around a warrior contrary to the sun, was not to be borne.

"Accepted," shouted Cúchulainn at him. "Come to the ford and learn your manners."

Down they went to the edge of the freezing river, from whose sluggish black water little wisps of fog rose here and there.

"This isn't my wish," said Cúchulainn when Etarcomol, sword drawn, shield rim level with his eyes, approached.

"You've no choice," said Etarcomol.

Cúchulainn stooped and his great sword whistled in the cold air. The cunning swift stroke cut the ground from under Etarcomol's feet, and he fell on his back.

"Home with you now," said Cúchulainn. "I don't want to have to wash my hands free of the slime of your guts."

"I won't leave," cried Etarcomol, white with fury. "Your head or mine. That's it."

"It'll be yours," said Cúchulainn. "For Fergus's sake I spare you." Two quick thrusts of the sword cut the straps that held Etarcomol's fine tunic, and the black garment fell to the ground, leaving Etarcomol naked in the icy wind.

"Off you go," said Cúchulainn.

"No," shouted Etarcomol in a fury.

The swishing sword now cut the hair off his head, and the beard from his chin. Still Etarcomol refused to admit he was overmatched. Then with one terrible stroke Cúchulainn split him in two from the crown of his head to the bones of his hips. The two sides fell apart, blood gushing on the snow. The death stroke was so fast that the entrails on each side were still moving as he fell split to the ground.

His charioteer, standing by the horses, leaped into the car and sped off, leaving me alone with Cúchulainn. For the first time he looked straight at me.

"I see a far-wandering man," he said. "What land do you seek?"

"My home is Ithaka."

"Take the homeward road then."

"Alas, that I cannot find," I replied.

"Nothing remains hidden that is eagerly sought," replied Cúchulainn. "He who cannot find his home has either offended the gods, or dares not venture down the road that leads to it."

"I would dare take any road that leads me to Ithaka," I replied.

"If that road leads across this river, you will not reach home, Wandering Man, except through the mercy of the gods."

"If the road leads across the river you guard, then I must cross whatever the cost," I replied.

At that moment Fergus came thundering back in his own great war cart. Three times in his fury he circled Cúchulainn left-handed in his chariot, and Cúchulainn stood humbly, head bowed, before the insult and challenge.

"Spawn of evil," shouted Fergus. "What disgrace you have brought on me! Do you think my sword powerless?"

"Ask the Wanderer what happened," said Cúchulainn.

"Etarcomol swore he would have my head. He left me no choice, though I tried to spare him."

"It is true," I said, and related what had happened.

"How could I best please you, Fergus my friend?" asked Cúchulainn. "Was I to let him take my head? Would that have pleased you more?"

"You did only what you had to do," said Fergus. "We have no quarrel. You have not dishonored me."

Then he made a spancel hoop and, taking the point of his spear, made a hole through the hocks of Etarcomol's feet. He passed the spancel hoop through both hocks and hitched the body to the back of his chariot.

"We leave," he said, and I jumped into the car. Away the chariot rumbled and rocked, over stony, frosty ground and over snowy, level ground. When the body came to the stony, frosty ground, the two halves dragged behind split apart, and the lungs and liver and kidneys fell out. And when they came to the snowy, level ground, the two halves came together again behind the chariot.

So glorious Achilles in my sight had passed a rawhide thong through a slit in the heels of Hector and dragged that proud warrior of the shining helm in the dust behind his chariot, tearing his strong limbs and battering his great bearded head to dogs' meat.

"Brutal treatment for a foster son of mine," said Medb when she saw the body.

"A boastful, ignorant dog, he was," said Fergus. "This sort of whelp should never pick a fight with such a Hound."

There was no more stone-throwing that night. Yet no one slept easily, for one among that host had now to face Cúchulainn at the ford. The six who had faced him up to that time had been slaughtered.

CHAPTER

21

ACH DAY MEDB CHOSE A NEW WARRIOR TO FACE
Cúchulainn and each day that man was slain. Soon,
no one wanted to challenge the guardian of the ford,
though Medb offered to each one of them her
youngest daughter Finnabair, the Golden-Haired.
A fine young plum she was, full breasted, slim waisted.
Medb, shameless as she was, had her appear fully clothed
before the warriors, to whom she gave copious drafts of wine,
and then divest garment after garment, with modest hesitation
(which the girl, though young, did to perfection). When there
remained only a white and flimsy tunic through which the full
nipples and wedge of fair hair were glimpsed, some warrior

would stand up and vow, all fire, to bring back the head of Cúchulainn the next day for such a prize.

"You are the expert in these matters," said Ailill. "Down they sit with one weapon and up they rise with two."

"Except Fergus and Uliseacht," said Medb.

"Other things could be tried," said Ailill. "No doubt you have thought of several stratagems. If not, I am willing to give advice."

"Will nothing cure you of your self-satisfied talk?" cried Medb. "It was exactly that fault, saying how fortunate it was for a woman to have a wealthy husband, that started the whole business. I think I could suffer a jealous husband more easily than a smug one." Her face became gorged with blood, so instant was her anger.

"I will never fight Cúchulainn, who is my friend," said Fergus. "Of that, whatever else happens, you can be certain."

"Great Queen," I added, "reflect that this war of yours is no concern of mine. It would not be fitting, then, to call upon someone unconnected with the war to help to win it for you, for the glory of your own victory then would be tarnished, and you would have to say that but for the valor of some stranger, your army could not have succeeded and obtained the great bull for you.

"Furthermore, consider also, that he who goes willingly into combat, having a deep interest in the outcome, either to promote his own glory or to avenge himself on an enemy, is twice armed. But he who goes into combat merely to oblige a friend or to return hospitality has no fire in his heart, and his sword arm then lacks a true smiting force."

"From Greece there are always honeyed words and half-done deeds," said Medb angrily. "Why have you avoided my warm bed each night? Truly you are a puny man. I think you prefer harping to wrestling and biting and thrusting."

These were shameful words to use of me before others, who

laughed at Medb's comments on my powers. So I thought secretly how I could avenge myself on her.

The list of warriors who fell victims in their lust for the firm breasts and body of Finnabair grew daily then. Nadcranntail, The Tree of Courage, fell first, spitted through the skull with a well-hurled javelin. Next Cur, son of the Two Champions, killed by a stone thrown through his head, then Lath, son of Two Waves, and Foirc, son of the Three Swift Beings, and Pig Snout, son of the Ever-living Yew. These were no small men, but the most famous warriors in the hosts of Ireland. Many more came after them. Daily came to the camp the beheaded body of some famous fighter, sliding about in his own jellied blood in the bottom of his chariot. The heads Cúchulainn kept.

"What does he need those heads for? Such a lust for heads is surely ignoble," I asked Dubthach, who could not be brought to volunteer to fight Cúchulainn either.

"Perhaps, like Conchobor, he makes a collection," said Dubthach. "It would not be unworthy if yours joined so famous an assembly," he added slyly.

"I pray the gods that I may safely carry my head back to Ithaka," I said.

"Between you and Ithaka are many obstacles—among them Cúchulainn," replied Dubthach. "Why do you hang back from a challenge? When are you going to meet him at the ford, Wanderer? Why not remove one obstacle which stands between you and your voyage home? As soon as this war is finished, you will be on your way home. Until then, you are caught here. Remember also, there is a reward for victory over the Warped One other than the prize of returning home —nothing less than the soft supple body of Finnabair struggling vigorously with you, who might well be the first man to receive the embrace both of her arms and of her thighs."

"Where is your own challenge, Dubthach?" I asked. "Come. Answer seriously. Is it friendship for Cúchulainn or fear that keeps you safe here in camp while we bury the headless bodies of your friends and daily erect great stones over them?"

Dubthach made no reply, but went off growling.

Each day, when these fearsome combats took place, the army was permitted to move while the fighting was on. In this way the Ulster boundary was forced. Farms and forests were raided and captives were taken. But time was short, for soon the warriors of Ulster would recover from their pangs and a battle to shake the whole of Ireland would certainly be joined. So Medb, having raided Ulster, thought better of it and withdrew across the river each time.

The men of the Galeoin troop distinguished themselves above the rest on these raids, though they had been divided up among the other troops of the army. They wore helmets of heavy bronze which covered their cheeks, leaving only slits for their eyes, very much in the style of the warriors of Lacedemonia, to whom they claimed to be related. They wore red cloaks which reached their waists over short blue tunics, and boots made of bear hide but covered on the sole with horse leather. These boots reached to their calves. Their favorite weapon was the short sword, but they were expert with the horse lance, the stabbing spear, the war ax and the sling as well. If the stockade of a fort was to be stormed, it was always one of the Galeoin troops first over the stakes.

And it was three of the men of Galeoin, who single-handedly captured the Donn Cuailnge—the brown bull over which the war had been launched.

They found the bull not at the farm of Daire, which they burned to the ground (a bitter sight for me to see so fine a place, like my own father's home, enveloped in smoke and flames). The bull had been taken to a valley in the hills, and it was the expert tracking of Ceth Fadceannach, the Fore-Sighted, of the Galeoin troop that traced him there. The tracking of the bull was in itself a tremendous feat, for a hundred heifers had been sent with him so that his big hoofprints were all but lost in the turmoil of prints made by the other cattle.

Five herders guarded the bull and the heifers in that lone valley. Two fled, two others were killed by the warriors of Galeoin, and the last was trampled to death under the hooves of the cattle he guarded when they stampeded over him.

Only the bull stood its ground.

There were a hundred men in the troop that found him, and he charged among them. His terrible horns impaled the fleeing men, who dared not stand before him. Twelve he killed until none would approach him but the three of Galeoin.

These stood alone, the rest having fled to the valley slopes, and awaited the charge of the bull. The great beast eyed them cruelly for a while, pawed the ground with hooves of iron, lowered his tremendous head and, with his tail lashing like a serpent behind him, prepared to disembowel them on his bloody horns.

Then the three noble warriors astonished all. They threw away their shields and, putting their swords in their left hands, draped their red capes over them like banners. Each moved apart from the other and the bull, with a roar that shook the valley, charged at the one in the center.

I thought him ripped apart when I saw the gory splash as the bull reached the warrior—Ferdia Ni Lachaedi his name. But instead, twirling aside like an athletic dancer, Ferdia escaped the sweep of the bull's horns, at the same time dangling his red cloak against the monstrous face of the huge beast. Then, marvelous to relate, he enchanted the divine bull with the red cloak, casting such a spell on it that the towering beast could do nothing but toss at the cloak with his horns, going around the warrior in a circle.

Complete silence fell upon the other warriors watching this. They had never beheld such a spectacle before. At last Ferdia drew a little away from the bull, which glared at him, bewildered, robbed of its powers, and then turned its gaze to another.

Down went his mighty head again. Again his tail writhed upward in fury, again he let out a bellow, pawed the frozen earth with his hooves and once more charged.

The charge was so furious that the earth where I stood, some distance away, trembled under the pounding of those iron hooves. Once more I thought the warrior killed in the flash of red as the bull thrust his horns upward. But he quickly sidestepped the sweep of those death-dealing horns, and the bull, unable to stop, swept by, leaving the man of Galeoin unhurt.

The bull turned, puzzled, lowered its head and charged again.

The same thing happened. The enchanted capes of the warriors utterly bewildered the divine bull of Helios. The others watching now cried out shouts of encouragement. At last, the three of them had the bull under such a spell that it meekly followed the red cape of Ceth Fadceannach, who had tracked it to this valley.

In this way, and by the men of the troop of Galeoin alone, was the Brown Bull of Cuailnge captured.

A great feast was celebrated over this tremendous victory. One thousand cattle were slaughtered, two thousand sheep and three thousand goats. Five hundred wild swans were killed, five hundred cranes and five hundred wild hares. A hundred great drinking vats were filled with wine and four hundred fifty with beer, and the whole army feasted and drank until not a man could hold a bite or a drop more.

The bull was of tremendous proportions—a true pet for Helios his master. He was half the size at least of that great wooden horse with which we Achaeans had tricked the men of Troy. His head was three times the height of the tallest man in the army of Connaught. His shoulders looked like the twisted trunks of two great trees, all knotted with muscles. His horns, black and gleaming, were each the length of a throwing spear, and his great eyes gleamed red in his noble head.

All were soon surfeited with food, beer and wine, and when the last of the carousers had fallen into a drunken, gluttonous slumber, I decided to put into effect a plan I had formed to avenge myself for the constant mockery of my manhood by Medb—and in front of others.

I found Finnabair, the golden-haired daughter of Medb, and invited her over to my chariot where she could lie with me under the covering stretched over the chariot pole and safe from all eyes.

"I cannot lie with you, Uliseacht," she said. "I must keep myself whole for whoever is victorious over Cúchulainn. However," she added, "the way things are going I am likely to die with my flower unplucked."

"It is a sad thing to see so lovely a girl as yourself offered only headless bodies for her bed," I said. "But do not fear that you will come to any harm at my hands, for I will not do one single thing to you or with you to which you do not readily assent."

"I do not know to what I would assent and to what I would not."

"It is time for you to find out," I replied. "At your age, you should know what are the boundaries to your behavior by proving them in action. Another consideration is this; you must lie with some man sometime. It is impious to deny yourself that great pleasure. Aphrodite will without a doubt visit you with some disfiguring blotching of your fair skin if you turn away from her delightful doctrines.

"That being so, it is better if you first lie with me who am a stranger and a wanderer and, as such, must be bound at every moment by discretion, rather than lie with one of these

((167))

rough warriors around, who, the moment they have enjoyed your embraces, will be boasting to others of what they achieved."

"I will come with you to your chariot, but I have not made up my mind to do anything at all," replied Finnabair. "Perhaps there is something you can teach me and I would be a fool to throw away an opportunity of learning from one who has traveled so far and may at any moment be gone from us."

"Good sense never led anyone astray," I said and, throwing my cloak over her, took her secretly to my chariot and under the hide covers which, thrown over the chariot pole, made a roomy tent below.

I had lit a fire in the entrance and the warm air had made the interior hot.

"It would be better if you modestly took off some of your clothes," I said. "That heavy embroidered cloak will make you sweat and you will be in danger of catching cold when I dutifully return you to your own sleeping place in a little while."

"I think you are right," she said, and removed her cloak, which she spread on the ground over the rough sheepskins which formed a covering there. The cloak was of green, and embroidered with gold.

"I often lie on it and think I am on a lawn of rich grass dotted here and there with yellow flowers," she said. Then she lay flat on her back on the cloak and said, "Tell me something of the lands in which you have traveled."

"I could tell you many tales of strange lands," I replied. "But there is an unexpected land which I long to visit at this moment and into which I ask you gently to guide me."

"Point out that land to me, Uliseacht," she said.

So I undid the fastening of her bodice and, putting my hands on her firm breasts, said, "These two young hills are the glorious gateways to that land. A slight valley runs between them to a delightful small pool set in alabaster. Beyond lies the golden mound of desire which above all else I would explore in that delightful country."

"Pass, Wanderer, and explore to your heart's desire," said Finnabair, and drew my bearded head down on her breast. So I kissed those lovely hills and traveled down the gentle valley to that smooth little pool set in alabaster and then, sending first some eager scouts ahead, traveled the golden mound and opened with gentle persuasion that entrance to treasure. In then, gently breaking the inner gate, and reaching ever further, received her treasure and gave her mine in return.

"Ah, Uliseacht," she whispered when we were done. "I feel with my trembling hands the wounds on your arms and back and thighs—wounds of sword and lance, borne in many bitter battles. I fear for you. Stay with me, Wanderer, and I will guard you from every harm. Fifty warriors will stand between you and danger, and I will love you to my last breath, for no man has ever moved me so."

"Fairest one," I replied. "How I wish I could stay with you and never move from where we are. But deep inside I hear the call of my home, my lovely farm, my strong and patient wife, Penelope, rich as the Earth itself, and I must go to her or die upon the way."

"Surely the gods love that woman that she should have you in her heart and she be in yours," she said. "Yet stay close to me a little while longer. These moments must last me through the burden of my life and bring summer to the winter ahead."

At this I wept that I had to leave her, though leave her I must.

She kissed away my tears and said, "Listen! Do you not hear now the music of lyre and of harp and feel the warm flower-laden summer air stir about us? The gods smile on us, Uliseacht, and give us treasure no one can destroy."

Then she put her golden head in the fold of my arms, and lying thus, we fell asleep.

((169))

CHAPTER

22

BEFORE LILY-FINGERED DAWN HAD TOUCHED THE eastern sky I awoke Finnabair lying in my encircling arms and, kissing her eyes in the intimacy of the dark, told her she must now return to her own sleeping place.

"No," she said. "I will not go to that grim prison but I will stay with you forever, for you have put a delight in my heart which no other man ever gave me or could give me."

"You are too young to use such a word as forever," I said, "and, as I told you, I am on my way homeward, to my own place and my own wife, Penelope. If the gods permit it I will some day find her and if they do not permit it, still I must struggle against them, seeking her to the last."

"I envy that woman and, except that you love her, I would fling a spear through her heart on sight," said Finnabair. "But since you love her then I must not harm her or hate her, but help you to reach her. But only give yourself to me again and pass tenderly through that country which you have made your own and which can never now belong to any other man."

So I drew her to me and she said, "I pray I may receive a seed from you into the rich earth of my womb. If fertile Cernunnos so wills it, what shall I call my son?"

"Call him Wanderer, for such he will be, as are all men," I replied.

Then I took her back to her own chariot, passing in the pale starlight the dark forms of bearded warriors sleeping with a leg or an arm thrown across their woman and around them the wan bones of the animals they had eaten. Death and birth carelessly lying so close to each other saddened me.

"Whatever happens this day," said Finnabair when we parted, "trust me, for I love you and am determined to help you."

"If you are in peril, one look or thought will bring me to your side," I replied. "I admit that I first thought to seduce you to avenge myself on your mother and her insults on my manliness. Yet you will have a shrine in my memory forever for the great loveliness you gave me this night, and I will think of you as a goddess and offer heart-sacrifices to you with each thought."

So we parted, and when the gray day came with a cold gleam of thin sunlight over the stark land, the army stirred itself and discovered that so careless had been their guard that the great bull had escaped during the night, for all had been drunk. When this news was received by the men of Galeoin they assembled and marched away, for they said truthfully that they had won the main prize of the war only to have their victory thrown away by the unsoldierly conduct of the rest of the army.

"Off with you then," said Medb. "I would sooner never have that bull than listen to you boasting forever that it was you who captured it."

I wondered then whether Medb herself had not secretly arranged for the bull to go free, for she could never stand the thought that anyone was better than herself and those at her command.

Later the war trumpet clattered its noisy summons and the warriors assembled to decide once again who was to challenge the man-destroying Cúchulainn on the following day.

"We have but to chop off his head and spill over all together into Ulster, find the bull, and the war is over," Medb said. "After all, Cúchulainn is very young and also he has been weakened by the many combats he has engaged in so far and which he has won only by the greatest good luck."

"Nothing will ever get the truth out of you," said Fergus. "And the truth is that there is not a man in the whole of Ireland who is a match for Cúchulainn in any style of fighting except myself."

"Then you should go and fight him, for you are in our service and you owe us that loyalty," said Medb.

"I will not fight him, for he is my foster son," said Fergus.

"I think it is fear of him and not fosterage that makes you say that," said Medb. "I would fight him myself, but it would surely shame the men of Ireland that a woman had to destroy single-handed the enemy they could not themselves defeat."

"You would get no nearer than a slingshot to him," said Fergus. "For he has sworn that at any sight of you, and at any time, he will send a death-dealing boulder in your direction."

"I would have been grateful if you had told me that before," said Medb. "I must be more prudent about the camp.

Let ten warriors hold their shields over my head when I am squatting. That is when women are most defenseless—men too, though they have an advantage in that they can stand. But I want you all to remember that whoever secures this last little victory for me—that is, brings me back the head of Cúchulainn—shall have the flower of my daughter, Finnabair, for his own, and my own friendly thighs on top of that to sweeten the bed and the bargain."

"That you cannot promise anymore," said Finnabair. "For I have already given that treasure to the warrior Uliseacht, who last night gently and lovingly plucked that bloom that flourishes only once in every woman. No doubt others can and will explore here and there about me, reaching the innermost recesses of my pleasant land, but every measure of that land belongs to him, for he was the first to enter it, and whoever follows will find that he has made it all his own."

"What is this disastrous thing you are telling me?" shouted Medb. "Have you really thrown yourself away on this worthless stranger when around you stand the strong and lustful warriors of Ireland?"

"His seed I have warm within me at this moment," said Finnabair. "With all my desire I nourish it."

"Well, there's an egg cracked we thought to keep whole for a while," said Ailill. "You'll never find a champion now. Standing cocks never weigh the consequences, but you'll find cooler judgments ruling from this day forward."

"Smug again," said Medb. "There's no curing you. You have a solution for every problem, but only after the damage is done. Well, who takes the prize must pay the price. That's plain sense. So Uliseacht must go against Cúchulainn tomorrow, and no argy-bargying. He's handy with sword and lance and club and maybe he can last an hour while the army gets to a better place. Maybe he knows a trick or two that might get him the victory."

"He could take a harper with him," said Fergus sourly.

"Why have you betrayed me?" I asked Finnabair. "You do not know what you are doing. It is impossible to kill Cúchulainn, and I have been warned against fighting him by the seer Fedelm, who is also a goddess. Not even gray-eyed Athena could help me in such a struggle."

But Finnabair only looked at me mildly and said, "Trust me, Wandering Man. Surely you know that I do not seek your death who have given me precious life to carry?"

"If it is not treachery then it is inexperience," I said. "You are too young to meddle in affairs of which you know nothing."

To this Finnabair replied, "The youngest woman is wiser than the oldest man, for wisdom is given to women with their birth, but men must argue and debate about it."

"Enough prattle," said Medb. "Off he goes. I am sure that there are enough of you around to see that he does not sneak out of what he has made his duty, plowing our little field by night and sowing his seed with abandon."

"That's a true word frankly spoken," said Dubthach. "I'll take him to the ford myself."

"What has happened to you, Dubthach, the Dark One, since you joined this army?" said Fergus, greatly surprising me. "I have been watching you. In the forays into Ulster you hold back. When the army marches you skulk behind. Your heart is not that of a warrior anymore, but that of a complaining farmer. Well, I will, as a favor, give you what your deeds in the past have earned you." With that he picked Dubthach up in his strong arms, held him over his head and threw him against a rock so that his skull burst and his bowels split open.

"Between you and Cúchulainn," said Medb, "we'll have no army left in a month. Now who is to see that the Greek goes to the ford?"

"I will," said white-haired Sencha, the Old One. "It is fitting at this time that I take him. He will not dishonor so old a warrior as I by cowardly flight."

"Why not Fergus Mac Roth?" asked Ailill. "He's the one who usually does this business."

"Because tomorrow I must burn the body of Dubthach with the arms he once bore in manly fashion and erect a stone over his grave," said Fergus. "He had become spiteful, but once his arm was as strong as any man's. It was exile from his homeland, which is Ulster, that spoiled him. The tree cut off from its roots rots and dies."

"You also are from Ulster, of which you were once king," said Medb.

"Perhaps I am dying too," said Fergus sadly. He glanced over at me. "How long are you away from Ithaka?" he asked.

"Twenty years," I replied.

"Twenty years. Certainly someone should help you return. I could not endure that," said Fergus.

"A man endures what a man must endure," said Sencha. "I will take my own chariot and my own charioteer tomorrow to the ford," he said. "That would be fitting."

"What sword will you carry?" asked Fergus warily.

"My own that I was given in my youth when I first took arms. None other than Fuilchicrach, the Blood-thirsty."

"It is a glory to me to say that I have fought many a time side by side with you, Sencha," said Fergus softly.

"I thank you for that and was myself honored to have had, on many dire occasions, so fine a comrade in arms," said Sencha.

They then placed each his hand over the other's heart, which among these barbarians is a gesture of trust and of parting.

23

N THE RIME FROST OF ICY DAWN NEXT DAY THE OLD ONE and I set out. On my way to the place where Sencha slept beneath his chariot I passed Finnabair standing in her cloak of dark green in the shivering dawn. She had thrown back her hood and her hair, a golden treasure, flowed over her shoulders.

"Your hair alone must serve to lighten the world this day," I said. "The sky is the shroud of the day."

"My heart leaps at the sound of your footstep, Wandering One," she replied. "In your land, think of me."

"I may never now reach my own land," I said, "but only

my death at the hands of Cúchulainn, with my head placed as Cathbad once half foretold, on a pillar in Conchobor's Gory House. Yet if that is not the case, I will remember you until the last beat of my heart sounds the call for me to descend among the shades and live as best I may in that eternal gloom."

"We have met before, Uliseacht," she said, "and will meet in memory again." Then she turned away.

She was gone in a moment, the green cloak turning darker with distance and then lost, never to reappear, in a deathly pall of ground mist.

"Don't gape there like a staggered sheep," said Sencha. "You may ride in my chariot, but not with that foolish look in your eyes. Arm briskly. There is warriors' work to be done."

"I am armed," I said, holding aside my cloak. "Sword, shield, helmet, it is enough for one who stood before Troy."

"Truly you do not enjoy fighting to so limit yourself in weapons," said Sencha. "Javelin, lance, club, double-bitted war ax and long-hafted war hammer—these used in turn delight the warrior and show his skill. To use sword alone is to call a man an athlete who merely walks fast and can neither run nor jump."

"Why are you so heavily armed?" I said, glancing at his laden chariot—a fearsome cart of black with blood-red scythe-encircled wheels.

"Cúchulainn has a gift for me," said Sencha. "I will require it of him."

At that he motioned me into his chariot, over the side of which hung his great shield of scarlet leather, ringed with heavy gold. Then with a cry of challenge he turned the chariot round right-handed in a salute to Helios, great chariot driver of the sky and giver of life.

Then off, with thick frost flung upward in smoke from the wheels as the lashing hooves of his steeds thundered over the frozen ground. A spray of frost flung upward also from those hooves, stinging the face fiercely and covering with a white coating the grim front of the war cart and the great pole between the plunging steeds.

Sencha, whose strong but withered arms handled bloody goad and reins in true warrior style, whose bushy eyebrows and thinning beard were soon frost clad, sang a war song, composed on the moment to the sorrowing skies and shroud-white land.

> *Here furious*
> *Loud singing,*
> *Goad-wielding*
> *Behind his*
> *Bloodflecked*
> *Steeds,*
> *Comes the Old One*
> *A meeting he keeps*
> *Of warrior kind*
> *With Him who*
> *Devours the earth.*
> *Down he goes*
> *Blood spattered*
> *Gut spilled*
> *Exulting.*
> *No shame*
> *Is to be found*
> *In such*
> *Defeat.*

At the ford, where the chariot flung spears of thin black ice from beneath its wheels, one-eyed Laeg, charioteer of Cúchulainn, stood waiting, combing his thick black hair, which crackled in the cold.

"I see two warriors," he said. "Which one seek Cúchulainn?"

"I seek him," said Sencha before I could speak.

"For what purpose, Old One?"

"That he may give me what is my due," said Sencha.

"If you wish to cross the ford, he will not stop you," said Laeg. "He honors you, Old One, and you may pass freely."

"It is not fitting that a warrior such as I should hold a long talk with a charioteer. Let him come forward and speak to me," said Sencha.

Cúchulainn then appeared, clad in his leather war coat, his deep-set eyes blazing and the war light shining about his golden hair—such was his appearance on this occasion.

"Old One," he said, "if there were but one breath of air left in the world I would get it for you and if the sky were to fall down and the earth to rise, I would hold them apart over the spot where you stand."

"That is well said," said Sencha. "For you have said to me that which I would also say to you. I would give you also the last glimpse of sight in my eyes before the blackness comes and the last ten beats of my heart that you might live a little longer."

"Many a red stag you taught me to bring down, Sencha," said Cúchulainn. "Many a cunning backhand blow of the war ax you gave on my behalf. What now can I do for you?"

"I come to claim a gift at your hands, Hound of Ulster."

"What gift is that?"

"A warrior's death," said Sencha. "I grow old. Soon the day comes that no man will fight me, claiming that it is dishonorable to fight one as old as I. Then there is nothing for me but to be eaten away by death as the worms eat an apple fallen in the grass."

"It would indeed be a dishonorable act for me to fight you," said Cúchulainn. "There is no honor to be gained from such a contest."

"I have earned the right of weapon-death," said Sencha. "That you cannot deny. What glory is there for you in denying that which is a warrior's due? Reflect also: I may still have a stroke which will catch you unguarded and permit me to take back your head to Medb. Nor would I claim Finnabair for my prize, for that has already been awarded."

"To whom?" asked Cúchulainn.

"To Uliseacht, the Wandering One," said Sencha.

Cúchulainn looked long at me. "Every prize you bear away either by cunning or by arms," he said. "Yet the prize of reaching again your own home is denied to you. Have you also come to challenge?"

"Sencha seeks to cross the ford between life and death in honorable fashion," I replied. "Say what is your judgment in that matter. Other things may be settled later."

"If I refuse Sencha his gift," said Cúchulainn, "will you then challenge me?"

"No. I will offer Sencha, if it is in my power, that which you refuse him—weapon-death."

Cúchulainn turned once more to Sencha. "Teach me again, Old One, what you know of arms," he said. "What weapon shall we try first?"

"The throwing javelin," said Sencha.

"Since you challenge, I must be the first to hurl the javelin," said Cúchulainn.

"To the ford then, you one side, I the other," said Sencha.

So they stood on opposite sides of that freezing, bubbling river which chattered over its rocky bed at the ford, though the deathly waters above and below were black with ice.

The javelins of Cúchulainn were hurled so fast that they might not be seen, but left a trail of frozen air behind them. The first Sencha deflected upward with his shield. The second he deflected down. The third he turned back so that it pierced Cúchulainn's unguarded shield arm. The fourth took out Sencha's eye.

"Well thrown," he cried. "You have gained in skill since

((180   ))

last we stood together against the Firbolg. Have you need of hazel ash for the wound in your arm?"

"I have not," said Cúchulainn. "Do you wish to stop, however, before you throw, while you bandage your eye?"

"No," said Sencha. "That would be unseemly."

Then he also threw and Cúchulainn easily turned aside the first three javelins, but Sencha cunningly lofted the fourth, which cleared the shield rim and struck Cúchulainn in the forehead, out of which scarlet blood flooded.

"What now?" cried Cúchulainn.

"Double-bitted ax," said Sencha. "Both to stand knee deep in the ford."

"Agreed," said Cúchulainn.

Thus they stood and swung mightily at each other with those terrible weapons, which made bright curves of light against the dark air. No shield protected those warriors wielding the limb-lopping axes. The water about them soon bubbled red foam. The arms of Sencha and the front of his war shirt were soaked in blood. Two fingers were gone from his shield hand, one dangling by the ligaments and tendons. Yet he did not flinch for a moment, but cunningly sliced the cheek of Cúchulainn open to the bone and, avoiding a blow aimed at his knees, laid open the muscles of his lightly armored back.

Loss of blood weakened them, and they drew off by mutual agreement to regain their vigor.

I cut off the dangling finger of Sencha, stanched the blood from the stumps with oxhide knots, and poured wine on the slicing wounds made in his arms and legs, from which the flesh hung in tatters. Then I gave him a deep drink of wine and begged him to refrain from further combat until his wounds could be properly dressed.

"You counsel like a child, Stranger," said Sencha. "Halfway to your home would you desist from your voyage, and not press all the more eagerly forward? So I am halfway over that ford which I must cross anyway. Let me go gloriously on."

When they had both rested and sent courteous and encouraging messages to each other, they met again, now with sword and buckler. With the permission of Cúchulainn, against whom Sencha would play no tricks, I tied the Old One's mutilated claw to the hand grip of his shield, and padded with frozen grass the stripped arm which must bear against the inside of it.

The fighting with swords did not end that desperate combat. Sencha lost his nose and an ear but Cúchulainn had his shield battered down with a rain of blows and at last cut in half so that the arm that held it was cut to the glittering bone. Then they were both weakened and withdrew to rest again.

"The old tree has the toughest knots," Cúchulainn called to Sencha.

"The young oak breaks the ax blade," replied Sencha courteously.

Rested, they returned to the fight of the ford, using the thrusting spear which they darted at each other from behind their great shields. At this work, Sencha proved the luckier, for receiving a great thrust of the spear in the upper part of the shield, below its heavy rim of gold, he twisted aside, wrenching the weapon from the hand of Cúchulainn, whose side was exposed for a moment.

Quick as a kingfisher Sencha darted his thin-bladed spear into the pit of Cúchulainn's arm. The spearhead came out, a tongue of blood, above the shoulder. That blow would have ended the combat had Sencha drawn his sword and with it lopped off the head of the Warped One, who fell back into the ford, the water piling over him in bubbling fury.

But the battle wrath now flared uncontrolled. Cúchulainn assumed a dreadful aspect. One eye disappeared inside his head and the other bulged huge and horrible in his face, like the Cyclops. He rose from the water, the muscles of his body wreathing about him like serpents gathering to crush. His mouth opened, with the lips peeling back to reveal his terrible teeth. He clenched his jaws and his teeth came together like the clash of shields. From the water, he snatched a spear thrown to him by his charioteer, Laeg. It was the terrible *gae bolga,* the belly spear which went in smooth as a needle but ripped out, barbs open. This he plunged into the body of Sencha, through his shield, kicking the butt of the spear with his foot. It pierced shield and belly and came out of the back of the Old One. Then Cúchulainn ripped the spear out again and Sencha fell, a gutted fish, into the ford.

"Farewell, Warped One," he cried. "I thank you for your gift." So he died.

Then Cúchulainn returned to the shape of a golden-haired boy warrior. He threw aside the belly spear and picked up the gore-covered body of the Old One. He carried the body across the ford and laid it on the grass, spiked stiff with frost. Then he fell across the dead man, fainting from his own wounds.

So Sencha made a warrior's crossing of the ford, not eaten away by worms, and his body was laid in his own land of Ulster from which he had been an exile ever since Conchobor's betrayal of Derdriu of the Sorrows.

CHAPTER

24

LAEG, THE CHARIOTEER OF CÚCHULAINN, CAME ACROSS the ford in the smoking cold air toward me. "You should let me have the war gear, cloaks and carpets of the Old One, so that his body may be burned with his warrior's trappings," he said.

"Take them," I replied. "But leave the chariot only, and the horse. These I need for my own use."

"Are you also to challenge the Hound?" asked Laeg.

"Why does he still protect the ford?" I asked. "Surely his days as champion should now be over, for the men of Ulster must by now have recovered from their pangs."

"He keeps the ford because the warriors of Ulster are still weak," said Laeg. "The labor of a woman in childbirth lasts a few hours at most. The labor of the men of Ulster lasts four days and five nights or five days and four nights. It is to be expected then that they must sleep for several days after that sterile laboring.

"You have not answered. Is it your warrior's duty to challenge Cúchulainn? Answer so I may tell him for whom to prepare tomorrow. You know that he is required to accept only one challenge each day."

"It is my duty but it is not one that I sought," I said. "It has been forced upon me."

"Tomorrow he will meet you," he said.

That night I slept beside the mocking shrill-voiced water of the ford, and between the great steeds, whose bulk could scarcely keep me warm. No one came from Medb's camp to visit me or to inquire whether I had been slain by Cúchulainn already. Before lying on the frozen ground I said a prayer to Poseidon, protesting that I was being forced to fight Cúchulainn, who from his terrible appearance before killing Sencha, I suspected might be the Cyclops or his son. Certainly at the ford they had resembled each other.

> Great shaker of the land and fish-filled seas,
> Brother of Olympus-ruling Zeus,
> It is Ulysses the Wanderer who calls,
> He who once escaped the Cyclops' cave
> Strapped beneath the purple-fleeced rams.
> All right. I blinded then your son
> And mocked him later from my lovely ship
> Silver-splashing in your wine-dark sea.
> That was wrong. But is it really right
> To judge a man by rules no gods obey?
> Consider, we are weaker than yourselves,

More prone to fault and vaunting boasts,
And for my moment's manly pride
Opposed I've been at every twist and turn
Upon the road to Ithaka, my home.
Now in this fearful island, gripped in ice,
That teeters on the shield-rim of the world
By tricks I'm called upon once more
To fling myself against another who may be
A son of yours—perhaps the same Polyphemos
Whose eye I burned out with hot fire
In his foul cave. Perhaps another.
Can I who whispered words of needed cheer
To trembling men within the Trojan horse
Now flee and so disgrace the bloodied arms
Of brave Achaeans fighting far from home?
Surely no god would ever favor me
After such a trick. Besides I'm not the man
To quail at odds. That you truly know.
Fight then I must but without enmity,
Bear that in mind. Take no revenge
For deeds in duty done. That's not right.
Withhold your wrath, for what I have to do
Honors Greece; does not dishonor you.

That was the prayer I said, and before I fell into a shivering sleep, a little sign was given that my prayer was heard. For casting about in my mind how best to fight Cúchulainn I hit on the scheme of enticing him to fight on land, not in the water, where surely a son of Poseidon must be at his strongest.

When bone-white dawn at last appeared I rose and, quickly crossing the ford, made my way to the camp of Cúchulainn.

"You're early," said Laeg.

"This may take a long while," I replied. "However, I am prepared to wait patiently if he needs more sleep to regain his strength for the test."

The words angered Cúchulainn. He was on his feet in a moment. "You are first here," he said. "Choose your weapon."

"Sword and shield," I replied. "No holding. No tripping with the feet."

"Agreed," he replied and, seizing sword and shield, flung himself on me. Easy to dodge that assault and without effort draw the sword edge across his face as he went by. But in that tremendous lunge of his all his wounds opened again on the moment. Blood spurted from every seam of his leather war coat and flooded over his hands and face. Still he turned and swung again a blow of which the wind was enough to knock me to the ground, though the blade itself missed. Up I got and found him fallen on the frosty grass, the battle light about his head dimming and at last gone, and his form changing from a fierce warrior to a boy hacked and mutilated by overwhelming odds. I had only to seize a handful of those golden curls and with one blow strike off his head to bring it back, jouncing against the side of my war cart, to the camp of Medb.

What man could resist such a triumph?

I took a handful of the bloodied hair, exulting, stretched the neck upright, swung back my arm for the victory blow. He looked at me, his blue eyes pale with death, and said those words I'd heard before when from my black-hulled ship I'd mocked the sightless Cyclops.

> *"Drowned in the wine of my wounds am I, Ulysses.*
> *Hold your hand. I'll treat you handsomely,*
> *Praying an offended god to be your friend.*
> *He is my father and will hear my words."*

As on a keen sword's edge, my resolution balanced—whether to strike off that head and be hailed the greatest champion of all Ireland, or whether, remembering Ithaka, to befriend him as I had not befriended the pleading Cyclops. One hair's weight could have turned the balance this way or that. He closed his eyes. The red blood welled more slowly between the caked black blood that had flowed before. I laid him down.

"No son can bind his father," I said. "But pledge that you will pray your own to withhold his wrath and let me hold again my dear wife in my arms, and feel again in my palms the fine warm, dry earth of Ithaka."

"The pledge is given," he whispered.

Then I called his charioteer and we carried that golden-haired one back to his chariot and, making all snug, dressed his wounds. I went myself across the ford and brought wine for this purpose. Laeg restitched his cut muscles with the split tendons of deer and stanched the bleeding with the ash of the sacred hazel tree. From a bag about his neck he took some of the berries of the mistletoe—divine plant which needs no roots in earth, but blooms in the air and in the dead of winter—and squeezed the juice between the pallid lips. Soon some strength returned.

"One further favor I will do you, Warped One," I said. "Since you have valiantly defended that ford out of your love of Ulster, I will stand guard for you, night and day, until you are well enough to handle your weapons, or until your lagging Ulstermen come to your aid. As you love your land, so I love mine, though long barred from its little streams and mountain meadows."

So I armed and went to the ford. But I found Fergus there already in glittering armor and carrying a mighty ax and keen long lance.

"Ask no questions, Wandering One," he said. "I defend here now until the Hound is well. Ulster is my kingdom, do not forget that. It is the duty of the king to defend his land and his people. Cross the ford again to your own side. It is your only chance to go home. Dally and you shall never again plow your own land."

Over then I went, the water deeper and deeper with every

step. I looked about, thinking I had mistaken my way, but the swirling black waters rose only higher and higher until with a bubbling rush they covered my head.

A light stole along the gray stones with their circles and lozenge carvings, picking out a sharp edge here, a hollow black as the eye socket in a skull there. It reached me and traveled up to my face and then down again.

"The rain is over now," said the farmer. "You can come out. It's a queer place to be without a light, and sleeping."

"What time is it?" I asked.

"Seven in the evening. You've been here a while. You didn't see anything?"

"Nothing."

"It's no place for sleeping," said the farmer. "There was one came down here once and never came out again. It's a place with one entrance and many exits."

CHAPTER

25

NEW YORK WAS FROZEN WHEN I RETURNED, AND the whole city alien to me. Muffled strangers scurried up and down the streets in tight silence between buildings which seemed themselves to exude cold.

The traffic noise was hushed by freshly fallen snow and the yellow taxis, swishing by, had a ghostly air as if they were things remembered from another life.

My own apartment seemed strange; the dwelling of someone I had once been and now looked on with compassion but with no real interest.

Circe was not in class when my lectures started again. I dragged myself through an alienated January and February, mouthing formulas about the early-nineteenth-century literary figures of England.

I met her just outside the university, on a budding day in March. She was standing under a maple which had the faintest mist of green here and there on its skeleton branches. A thin sunlight seemed to surround her, and when I saw her, my heart leaped.

She was holding a huge stack of books. I took them from her and she said, "You look lost."

"I am," I said. "Utterly and completely lost. Frozen into a block of ice. Surrounded by strangers and in a foreign place and the wrong time. When I speak, people don't seem to be listening. When they speak, I'm not listening. Can you come with me?"

She gave me a troubled look, hesitated and said, "All right."

We bought some groceries, brown bread, wine, cheese and liverwurst. The things we had bought before. My apartment was freezing. She picked up the telephone, called the building superintendent, and told him we needed more heat. My own complaints on that subject had always been met by platitudes about the fuel shortage. We got heat immediately. Then she tidied everything up and made up my neglected bed, putting on the sheets with the small yellow roses.

"Let's make love," she said quite simply. She unzipped her jeans and slipped them off, then unbuttoned her blouse, revealing the chalices of her breasts, and struggled out of her white panties, which she kicked off her ankle with one graceful swing of her foot.

The touch of her flesh was like summer again. I felt alive, all the care and wrinkles gone.

She put her hand gently behind my head and pulled my face down to her breasts. "Poor Wanderer," she said. "So very far from home."

Later, while we ate, I told her about Ireland, but she did not seem to be listening. Or rather she seemed like someone who was hearing what she already knew, but it would be impolite not to listen. When I talked of Fedelm and Finnabair she smiled a little, but whether it was because of my confessing my lovemaking with them or for another reason I could not decide. Nor could I bring myself, for fear of breaking some enchantment, to question her directly about them and herself.

When I had done she said, "I dropped Western Lit and

took Spanish instead. You know there are a lot of Spanish-speaking people in New York. It's a shame how they are ignored. And we have a really exciting teacher—Ramon Monez. He's from Cuba. Sort of an exile. Far from home."

My heart sank.

"How are you doing—how are your grades?" I asked.

"Well, I was getting *F*'s," she said, "but I'm getting *A*'s now. You know how it is."

"Yes," I said. "I know how it is."

She didn't stay with me. That last act of love was a farewell gift and a setting of me free. She had found someone else in need of a goddess. When she left she said, "You really ought to get out of this freezing place. You ought to go home. Don't bother about me. Just go home where you want to be."

I left the university at the end of that quarter. I sold everything I had and took a ship to Brindisi, and then a ferry to Corfu and then another ferry to Ithaka. An old hound asleep in a shadow shuffled toward me when I landed at Vahti. People watched him and eyed me closely and then went on with their talk. The hound followed me around, stumbling on his worn limbs, happy when I gave him a pat, content at night to return to the pile of dung on which he slept, with only flies and memories for companions.

It was a week later that I found Penelope. She was coming down a street of steps, her hair gray, her face beautiful but worn with waiting. The hound panted breathless at my heel. I knew her immediately.

"You have been a long time away," she said.

"A hundred thousand years," I replied. "I will not go away again."

I hope it is true. Sometimes now I sit watching the wine-dark sea and hear the thump of oars against thole pins, see the heaving muscles of the men, and hear the rush of the silver-crested waves and the cry of the helmsman. Then Penelope looks at me with wise, sad eyes and goes quietly away.